SUMMER
WOLVES
OF THE

We want to hear from you. Please send your comments about this book to us in care of zreview@zondervan.com. Thank you.

ZONDERKIDZ

Summer of the Wolves
Copyright © 2012 by Lisa Williams Kline

This title is also available as a Zondervan ebook.
Visit www.zondervan.com/ebooks

Requests for information should be addressed to:
Zonderkidz, 5300 Patterson Ave., SE Grand Rapids, Michigan 49530

ISBN: 978-0-310-72613-5

Library of Congress Cataloging-in-Publication Data

Kline, Lisa Williams, 1954-
     Summer of the wolves / by Lisa Williams Kline.
       p. cm. — (Sisters in all seasons)
     Summary: While vacationing on a horse ranch in North Carolina, stepsisters Stephanie and Diana put aside their differences to help free a pair of caged wolves.
      ISBN 978-0-310-72613-5 (hardcover)
     [1. Stepsisters—Fiction. 2. Stepfamilies—Fiction. 3. Wolves—Fiction.
4. Animals—Treatment—Fiction. 5. Horsemanship—Fiction.] I. Title.
PZ7.K67935Su 2012
[Fic]—dc23   2011052826

Cover design: Kris Nelson
Interior design: Sarah Molegraaf

Printed in the United States

---

12 13 14 15 16 17 18 19 20 /DCI/ 18 17 16 15 14 13 12 11 10 9 8 7 6 5 4 3

SISTERS IN ALL SEASONS

SUMMER
OF THE WOLVES

BY LISA WILLIAMS KLINE

ZONDER**kidz**

ZONDERVAN.com/
AUTHORTRACKER
follow your favorite authors

CHILDREN'S LIBRARY

DIANA

y pills always made me sleep in the car. And they gave me crazy dreams. We were on the highway, and I dreamed I was riding this speed demon of a horse—like Man o' War. As the dream went on I realized I wasn't riding, I *was* the horse. I *was* Man o' War, and it was the greatest feeling. Galloping, galloping out ahead of everyone. And then there were other horses breathing really loud all around me. And then we were running up a steep mountain. Rocks slipped under my hooves, bouncing downhill. I lost my footing. The other horses were leaving me behind.

I jerked awake. The car went around another switchback, heading almost straight up. My ears popped. I swallowed, trying to get them to stop. Norm, my stepfather, turned off the air conditioner and hit the button to roll down the windows. Cool air flowed in. I rubbed my hand over my eyes. "Are we at the ranch?"

"Diana, you're awake!" Mom turned and smiled. "Yeah, we're almost there. And look, girls." She pointed to spiky bushes with delicate pink and white flowers clinging to the cliff beside the road. "Aren't the mountain laurel beautiful?"

"Ooh, yeah, they are," said Stephanie, giving Mom that fakey Southern girl smile.

I glanced at my new stepsister's polished toes, her sequined flip-flops, and tanned, smooth legs. Then I looked at my own scuffed leather sandals and worn jeans. The only thing Stephanie and I had in common was that we were both about to start eighth grade. Stephanie acted so perfect. It had to be a front. Who could be that sweet?

"Diana and Stephanie, look! Riders!" Mom pointed at five people on horseback who had just come around the corner. They faced us on the skinny gravel road.

Horses! I yanked off my seat belt and stuck my head

and shoulders out the window. The horses were so close I could hear the clop of their hooves on the path and the squeak of the saddle leather. First in line was a white Appaloosa with black flecks on his haunches. The last was a little chestnut with a black mane and tail. He was out in the road trying to edge past the pony in front of him. Just as our car got close, the pony kicked the chestnut. The chestnut reared. The rider screamed and wrapped her arms around his neck.

Norm slammed on the brakes.

"Hey!" I grabbed the edge of the window and just about fell out.

"Whoa!" The leader stopped the Appaloosa and turned in her saddle. She was a dark-skinned woman with a bushy gray braid sticking out from under a stained cowboy hat. "Copper doesn't like to be last," she said. She got off her horse and said, "Copper!" Then she made a strange sweeping motion with her arm. The chestnut calmed down right away. "You can go ahead," the woman said to Norm, and tipped her hat. Then, as she remounted, she said to the riders behind her, "Everybody okay? We're almost back to the barn."

I kept on leaning out, watching the riders. How had that weird-looking woman calmed that horse down with just a sweep of her arm? I realized Mom was telling me to get back into the car. "Oh, man, I want her for my trail leader! And that's the horse I want to ride!"

"You've got to be kidding!" Stephanie said. "That horse bucked with that girl on its back!"

"It did not buck," I said. "It reared."

"It was standing on its hind legs." Stephanie's face had a look of terror.

"That's not bucking. You don't even know what bucking is."

"Diana!" Mom cried.

"Well, she obviously doesn't know anything about horses," I said. I lowered myself back inside.

Mom narrowed her eyes at me, put her finger on her temple, and tapped it twice. The signal suggested by my shrink. It meant, *Take a deep breath and think before you blurt things out.* Mom was supposed to signal me without embarrassing me in front of other people. It seemed okay when Dr. Shrink first mentioned it. But now I felt like your basic trained dog.

Mom smiled at Stephanie. Then glared at me. "Diana, why isn't your seat belt on?" Mom watched me until I buckled my seat belt, then she put her hand on Norm's shoulder and squeezed. "This mountain driving is nerve-racking, isn't it?"

"Well, especially when there are hordes of wild beasts in the middle of the road," Norm said, grinning at Mom. "I hope you know what you're in for, Lynn, dragging a city boy up here to the mountains. Please tell me they have indoor plumbing."

"Oh, gosh, Norm, don't tell me you forgot to bring corn cobs for the outhouse?"

Norm's eyes got wide. Mom started laughing.

Norm pretended to bang his head on the steering wheel. "What was I *thinking*?" Stephanie and Mom laughed. Her hand was still on Norm's neck. I felt like biting it.

Last week Mom had dragged me to Dr. Shrink's office. We have a new family now and we all have to try to get along. Blah, blah, blah. The problem these days was Mom spent all her time trying to make Norm and Stephanie happy. Norm with his pocket calculator and stupid jokes. Stephanie with her rainbow toes and bouncy dark hair. Apparently Miss Congeniality at her school. Doesn't have to take mood pills. I felt like that little chestnut pony—last in line.

I stared out at the shadowed forest as we wound up the mountain. If I were an animal, I'd jump out of this car, run into the woods, and keep right on running for miles.

Except, there was the chestnut pony. The lady called him Copper. I figured I could get him to like me. I knew it.

Norm shifted gears. The engine growled low, like a bear. "Call me cynical," he said, "but I have a feeling my cell phone is not going to work up here."

"Who would you need to call, anyway?" said Mom. She gave Norm a flirty smile.

Ugh.

Then we reached the top of the mountain and wow, High Mist Ranch spread out before us like a wavy quilt, its pieces edged with fences and horse trails. Horses and cattle grazed in sloped green pastures dotted with purple and yellow wildflowers and white chunks of rock salt. The rustic lodge looked out over the green valley, with purple mountains layered in the distance. Winding riding trails climbed up a ridge where you could see the Smoky Mountains for miles in every direction. I could hardly breathe, it was so beautiful.

"I have to ride today!" I said.

"We can definitely ride tomorrow," Mom said. "It might be too late today. Isn't this beautiful?"

"Gorgeous," said Norm. "You told them we wanted the unit with the hot tub and the espresso machine, right, babe?" Stephanie and Mom both laughed.

The minute Norm pulled up beside the lodge, I jumped out and headed in by myself. The lodge was made from huge dark-colored logs that must have come from trees two hundred feet tall. Inside, the ceiling had giant beams made from those same logs. In the front room to the right was a desk where people checked in. To the left stood a stone fireplace, a soft-looking leather couch, and a thick rag rug thrown over the stone floor.

Mom and Stephanie came in. Mom put her arms around both of us. "This place looks nice, huh?" When Stephanie snuggled up to Mom, I escaped into a dining room with two long wooden tables. At the far end was the biggest fireplace I'd ever seen, with a stone face and heavy wooden mantel. A fire crackled, even though it was the middle of July. In front of the fireplace was a low coffee table with a Monopoly board set up with money and game pieces. No one was playing. No one was here at all.

Movement flashed through a window beside the fireplace and I stepped closer. Three bluish-green hummingbirds darted around a feeder. Their wings were a blur, kind of sparkling. I sat in the window seat and watched them flit, drink, and zip away. Imagined holding up my finger and one of the hummingbirds landing on it.

I'd never admit this to anyone, but I'd always wanted to be like those characters in old Disney movies who had animals following them around. Like Cinderella and her mice. Whenever I walked into a barn, I imagined all the horses swinging their heads to look at me and all this love pouring out of their big-as-the-world eyes. Animals knew things about me that people never seemed to understand.

Past the feeder, just a few hundred yards down the hill, I spotted the barn. The little chestnut, tied to the corral fence, pawed at the ground and twitched his tail, waiting for someone to unsaddle and groom him. He wasn't content like the others. My heart squeezed. I knew exactly how he felt, just like he'd spoken to me.

A kitchen door that read "Staff Only" swung open. Two people came out, talking. They didn't see me in the window seat. One of them was the woman I'd just seen on the trail with the long gray braid. She still wore her riding boots and an ancient flannel shirt.

"Here, this is about five pounds," whispered a guy with a ponytail. He handed a greasy package to the woman with the braid. Wiped his hands on a blood-stained white apron.

"They'll finish that off in ten seconds." The woman had a deep gravelly voice almost like a man's. Her gray hair was matted down where her floppy hat had been.

"One of these days you're going to lose a hand feeding them," said the guy.

"I'm careful." The woman patted the guy's arm. "Thanks." She left the lodge with the package, and he ducked back through the swinging door into the kitchen.

Horses didn't eat meat. What was that woman feeding that would eat five pounds of meat in ten seconds? And might bite her hand off?

"Diana!" Norm leaned through the doorway. "Come on, we're all checked in, let's go find our cabin." When I got to the doorway, he put his arm over my shoulders in a stiff hey-we're-pals sort of way. "It's too late to sign up for a trail ride today, but at dinner we can sign up for first thing tomorrow morning."

"Okay." I made my voice sound bored. Norm acted like he cared about me, but there was no way he could care about me as much as my own dad. And if things started to totally go downhill, I'd move to Florida with Dad.

Through the window, I saw the woman with the package get into an old black truck. She backed up, the tires crunching over gravel, and then headed down the mountain, kicking up a swirling cloud of red dust.

I left the dining room and followed my so-called family out to the car.

2

STEPHANIE

I followed Diana up some rickety stairs to the loft bedroom we'd be sharing this week. Now that I saw this place I could see why Daddy kept joking around about the hot tub and espresso machine. The cabin had an A-shaped ceiling, and the inside walls didn't even have any paint on them. They were this rough yellowish wood with scattered brown knots that looked like a bunch of bull's-eyes in different sizes. If Mama saw this place? Honestly, she wouldn't even unpack her bags.

I leaned over the loft railing and saw the sofa below, covered with a ratty old Indian blanket. "Hey, check it out," I said, hoping Diana and I would get to talking. "We can look down over this railin' right into the livin' room. Hey, we can drop water balloons on Daddy and Lynn if they try to make out or anything."

"Who cares if they make out?" Diana's eyes, when she looked at me, were kind of mocking.

"Not me, just kiddin'," I said, real quick. "So, which bed do you want? You can pick first." I was starting to feel real disappointed because I'd hoped Diana and I would get along. I mean, if we got along, this week could be so much fun.

"I'll take the bed by the wall." Diana heaved her suitcase onto the bed and dumped it out. She hardly had any clothes. There were three pairs of jeans, two sweatshirts, a few T-shirts, a pile of underwear, and about ten pairs of rolled up socks.

I brought an outfit for every day. And some of mine—not *all* of mine, but some—had good labels. Mama *loves* labels. Before Daddy married Lynn, she and Diana had lived in a condo in a neighborhood that Mama said was on the wrong side of the tracks. Before this trip Mama had even said a couple things about Lynn and Diana that in my humble opinion might fall into the category of "catty." But Lynn had been really sweet to me and I always agreed more with Daddy's way of looking at things. That is, you shouldn't judge people by their stuff.

Daddy had said to try to be patient with Diana. Diana had to take some kind of medicine. Daddy had sat down with me before we came and we'd talked about being loving and understanding. "Gettin' along with people is easy for you," he had said. "But not for her." I was going to try to do what he said.

"I'm taller, I'm taking the top drawer." Diana grabbed her pile of clothes and stuffed them into the drawer. A few socks and pairs of underwear fell on the floor. She threw a book on her pillow and left her empty suitcase on the bed.

Well, that was kind of rude. And the way she was throwing stuff around was really getting on my nerves. I took some deep breaths. I found the Tums that Mama hid in my suitcase and popped one in my mouth.

Keep being nice, the way Daddy said. Make conversation.

I closed the drawer Diana had left open and stacked my own shorts, camis, and T-shirts in the bottom drawer.

"So," I pointed at the book on the bed. "Is Man o' War a horse?"

"*Was* a horse. He's been dead about a hundred years."

Diana sat on the bed and kicked off her sandals. One landed on the bed, and the other flopped on the floor.

"He must be pretty famous."

"Duh." She pulled out these disgusting worn-out cowboy boots (mine were brand new red leather) and sat on the bed to put them on.

I tried again. "Maybe I could read it after you finish."

"After I finish I'm probably going to start it again. I've read some parts six times." Diana had two pairs of those heavy socks on and she was shoving her left foot down into one of the boots.

"Oh." *Now what?* I kind of felt like crying, so I turned around and started lining my lotions and nail polishes on one side of the dresser. "I'll keep my stuff on this side."

"Take the whole thing, I don't care," Diana stomped on the floor to shove her foot down into the boot. When her boot heel hit the floor, it sounded like someone hammering.

"Hey!" Daddy's voice drifted up the stairs. "Somebody doing carpentry work up there?"

Diana kept right on stomping.

Real slowly, I pulled my new jeans from the bottom of my suitcase. They had patterns of sparkly multicolored rhinestones on the pockets and seams. I'd begged Mama to buy them for the trip. "Will these be okay for riding?" The minute I said it I knew they weren't.

Diana snorted. "Only if you want everybody at the barn to laugh their heads off."

I turned around and put the jeans back in the drawer so Diana wouldn't see my face. "Well," I said after a minute. "Maybe I just won't ride."

Diana stood with one boot on and her other foot halfway into the other. "What the heck will you do all day?"

I shrugged. At art camp last summer, there had been drawing in the morning and painting in the afternoon. I'd loved sitting at the pottery wheel after dinner with my fingers caked with cool gray slip, listening to my iPod, getting lost in the music. "Lynn said they might have a pottery or quilting class I could take."

"Quilting? What are you, like, an old lady? And why do you call my mother 'Lynn,' like you're good friends with her or something?"

I sure wished Diana would quit trying to pick a fight. Who did she think Daddy and Lynn were trying to make happy when they came to a ranch, anyway? Daddy must have totally forgotten about that time three years ago when I fell off that horse and dislocated my shoulder. When that doctor shoved my shoulder back into place I thought I'd faint dead away from the pain. Nobody had asked *me* if I wanted to come to a ranch for our vacation. Because if they'd asked me, we'd be at the beach lying in the sun one day and going shopping the next.

"Well, I thought you'd be mad if I called her 'Mama.'" I kept my voice even. "Besides, I already have a mama."

"What about evil stepmom?" Diana made a face, then fell back on the bed, stuck her foot straight up in the air, and pulled on the bootstraps with a huge loud groan.

Maybe it would be a good idea to change the subject. "Hey, I can French braid your hair if you want. My friend Ally taught me."

Diana started stomping again. "Are you kidding? You do that and my hair will end up looking like stalks of straw in a rubber band."

"I bet it looks great. C'mon, I'm good at it."

"Nah." With one more grunt, Diana shoved her right foot into the boot. "I'm going to the barn!"

"I thought you couldn't ride until tomorrow."

Without answering, Diana tripped down the stairs and out the screen door, letting it slam behind her.

"Fine, don't invite me; I don't want to go to that dirty ol' barn anyway," I said to the empty room. People in my youth group at church talked about having stepsisters and stepbrothers. They said sometimes it's hard to get along, but I liked to think that I could get along with just about anybody. Moving all over the south because of Daddy moving up at the accounting firm had taught me how to find places to fit in. But you'd have to walk around wearing a halo to get along with Diana.

I went in the bathroom, stepping over Diana's clothes, and pulled my hair into a ponytail. I'd thought a lot about how weird this vacation might be. When Daddy used to live in our same house, he went to work and back and hardly noticed me except to pat me on the head once in a while. Now it was like he went out of his way to pay attention to me. Because of everything going on in the family, there was this *pressure. Pressure to be perfect.*

Like when you blow a big bubble with those little plastic wands, it looks so shiny and perfect, with the rainbows reflecting, but it's nothing but a thin film of soap. Any minute it could pop.

After I lined up my hairbrush and toothbrush and barrettes, I tried to ignore Diana's sandals on the floor, but then I picked them up and put them in the closet by her bed. Downstairs, Daddy and Lynn were still unpacking. I told them I was going to look around, and they (naturally) suggested that Diana and I go together. I told them Diana had already headed over to the barn. Apparently they were preoccupied when she slammed the screen door.

"I'm being patient with Diana," I told Daddy when Lynn went outside to dump the ice from the cooler. "*Extremely* patient."

Daddy draped his arm across my shoulders and pulled me close to him. "Hey, come on, sport. It's only the first day. You have to give these things time."

"Oooh-k-a-ay," I said, making it sound like it was going to be a lot of work. I headed outside our cabin door and followed the gravel path toward the lodge.

This fall I would start living with Daddy every other week and go to Diana's school. He was fixing a room for me in their new house, and he said we'd have a party so I could get to know people. I could tell Diana didn't want to. Diana was a year older than me, but we'd both be in eighth grade. Daddy said Diana had to repeat third grade when she changed schools after her parents got divorced. He said for me not to make a big deal about that. That kind of hurt my feelings. How could he even think I'd do that? Especially when I know how it feels to go through a divorce.

As I approached the lodge, I saw three oak trees spreading a big old blanket of shade around them. Under one of the trees this tanned boy with spiky, light-colored hair was throwing horseshoes all by himself. He was skinny. Super-skinny, and I heard Mama's voice in my head, *"He'd have to run around in the shower to get wet.*" As I walked by, the boy threw a wild shot that flew over the stake and hit the path in front of me.

"Hey, grab it!"

I reached for the horseshoe and missed, and it started tumbling down the hill. The boy ran in front of me, practically *colliding* with me, and finally caught the horseshoe when it slowed down and fell flat.

He walked over and gave me a big old grin. "What can I say? I'm not on the Olympic horseshoe team." He gave his head a little toss and rolled his eyes. "Actually, I don't even know if horseshoes *is* an Olympic sport."

I laughed. "No."

"Oi say, old chop," he said, faking an English accent. "Could I interest you in a game?" He was looking at me like he couldn't stop smiling.

"Well … I guess so." I put my hands in my back pockets, following him up the hill to the horseshoe pit. He was pretty cute. "But you have to teach me."

"Splendid!" he said with the fake accent again, then switched back to his regular voice. "Hey, it's not rocket science."

His name was Nick. He taught me to pitch the horseshoe underhanded in the direction of the stake. After he threw two in a row right around the stake, a lightbulb went on in my head.

"Hey, did you throw that horseshoe at me on purpose?" I put my hands on my hips.

"No way!" He gave this twitch and threw a horseshoe in the complete opposite direction of the stake. "Oops."

He held his hands out in a *What can I say?* gesture, and I couldn't help laughing at his goofy grin. We kept on playing, and after a couple turns I got a horseshoe close enough to earn one measly point. I found out Nick was an only child and was at the ranch by himself with his parents. Then I asked what I really wanted to know.

"Are you a good rider?"

"No way," Nick said.

"You're probably just saying that."

"Seriously," Nick said. "I've only been horseback riding once in my entire life and that time I got on the horse backward." Nick's mouth twitched when he said this. He had exactly five freckles on his nose.

"I saw that twitch!" I couldn't stop laughing.

All of a sudden the week was starting to look like a whole lot more fun.

DIANA

My boots made scuffing noises and stirred up puffs of orange dust as I headed down the hill to the barn. Stephanie and Mom could go make a pot holder together. They could knock themselves out.

During Mom and Norm's honeymoon, I'd gone to Florida and stayed with Dad and his girlfriend, Susan, and got to hang around their apartment every day. Dad said next visit maybe he'd take a day off work and we'd go to Sea World. Dad didn't nag me about my pills like

Mom and Norm did. He never nagged me about what I had for lunch. Whether I'd taken a shower. I'd basically done whatever I wanted.

Twice last month I texted Dad to see if I could come stay the rest of the summer. When I turned fifteen next month I could get a work permit. But I hadn't heard anything back. Why hadn't Dad texted me back?

Mom said Norm really cared about me. She said that when someone reminded you to eat breakfast and take your pills or not to interrupt people's conversations, it meant they cared about you. Blah, blah, blah. I know the pills make me calmer, but they make me feel so tired and boring. Like I have no feelings. Sometimes I'd rather be mad.

When I got close enough to the barn I breathed in the smells of clean hay, the polished leather saddles and harnesses. One of the horses inside nickered softly. Maybe it was Copper, saying hello.

There was something about that horse. I couldn't wait to ride him.

Horses didn't ask questions like, "How are things going at school right now? Are you feeling more able to control yourself these days?" Horses took you for who you were. My shrink came up with this thing where I'm supposed to pick a number for my mood between one and ten. One being basically catatonically calm, i.e., dead. Ten being totally hyper and ready to self-destruct in ten seconds. Five being where you want to be. I call it the Moronic Mood-o-Meter. Anytime I'm anywhere near a barn, I'm a five.

Two barn kittens were playing by the barn gate. One was tiger-striped and the other was black with a white face and paws. They were so cute! On a low stone wall beside the fence slept a big tiger-striped mother cat. One of the kittens jumped up on the wall. He shoved his little nose into the loose fur of her stomach, trying to nurse. With one swat of her paw, the mother cat knocked the kitten off the wall. The other kitten jumped up and tried to nurse. The mother just stood up and left. The poor kitten dangled from her teat as she walked away, dragging him for a few steps. Then he fell off the wall too. Both kittens tried to climb the wall to try again, but the mother ran away.

"Do you have a mean mom?" I sat on the wall and scooped them both up. They mewed, high-pitched, and their tiny pliable claws pricked my skin. Their noses were pink and moist. I held them for a few minutes, feeling their small warm chests vibrate as they purred. Then they jumped from my lap and ran off looking for their mother again.

I ducked through the barn door. Waited for my eyes to adjust to the darkness inside. The barn was laid out like a "T," with the tack room and the office at the top of the T, and the stalls in rows at a right angle. Beams of light streamed through windows above the stalls, making the place seem kind of heavenly. A woman was in the office behind a glass window on the phone. Otherwise I had the barn to myself. I turned the corner and headed down the aisle between the stalls, looking for the little chestnut.

Most of the horses were eating and only cocked their ears when I walked by. At the end of the row on the right, one head poked over the door of a stall.

It was him! I caught my breath when I saw his beautiful face. He had to have some Arabian in him. I'd read that Arabians could go up to five days without water because of their desert heritage. When I got close, he tossed his head. I remembered to slow down and talk to him quietly.

"Hey, there, Copper, buddy, what are you doing? You are such a pretty boy! Yes, a very pretty boy."

He watched me come closer. His eyelids kind of closed. I held my palm out for him to nuzzle. Shoot, why hadn't I remembered to find some sugar or a carrot? His muzzle was so soft, but he was nervous. I tried stroking his forehead, but he snorted and tossed his head.

Head shy.

I held my palm still, kept talking. He snorted again,

then walked to the back of his stall, but he turned to look at me. A good sign.

I talked some more. "You don't trust me, do you Copper? It's okay. It's hard to trust people."

Copper took a step toward me, stopped, and tossed his head.

"I would never hurt you. You seem a little wild, but I can tell you're a very sweet boy." Copper walked slowly across the stall. Put his head over the gate. Let me scratch between his ears.

4

STEPHANIE

Right around sunset somebody rang a cowbell, and we headed over to the lodge for supper. The wooden tables in the dining room had silverware laid out on red checked napkins and big old pitchers of iced tea. As we walked by the salad bar, I saw Diana grab a handful of carrot sticks and shove them in her jeans pocket.

"What are you doing?" I asked.

"I'm going down to see a horse at the barn later."

Lynn slid into a chair near the end of one of the long wooden tables. Daddy was getting ready to sit next to Lynn, but then Diana plopped herself in that chair, so Daddy sat across from Lynn and I took the seat beside Daddy.

Other people were filing into the dining hall. I looked for Nick but didn't see him. The lady we'd seen before with that gray braid came up. Mama had always told me that when women reached a certain age they ought to cut their hair. The lady's face was lined, and her hands were real red and wrinkled. Mama would call her a candidate for a complete makeover. More "catty" talk. But I thought the lady had a nice face, with laugh lines at the corners of her eyes. I liked her right off. "Good evenin'," she said. "I'm Maggie, the head wrangler." I liked the sound of her voice, a country accent that was both twangy and poetic. Southern, but different from the way Daddy and I talked. "So, everyone's ridin' tomorrow morning, right?" she asked.

Riding? Her question was so sudden I thought I might faint.

"I'm riding!" Diana jumped up and stuck her hand right in front of Maggie's face, like some rude little kid. "I want you for my trail leader. And I want to ride Copper."

Maggie's brown eyes widened, and she gave this

gravelly chuckle. "We'll see what we can do, darlin'. What's your name?"

"Diana. And I'm an advanced rider. I've been taking lessons for three years."

Diana was advanced! Even worse than I thought.

"That so," Maggie said. She looked at Diana a minute, then didn't say anything else.

"She's intermediate," Lynn said.

"Okay. What about you, darlin'?" She looked at me.

Before I could answer, Daddy said, "The girls can ride together."

I looked down at my plate. Why did Daddy always do this? It was almost like he was doing it on purpose.

"You've taken lessons?" Maggie was still talking to me.

"Yes, she has," Daddy said.

I stared at Daddy and started to say something, but clamped my mouth shut, feeling my cheeks go hot as a jalapeño pepper.

"My wife signed us up for the adult trail ride," Daddy went on. "I'm a city slicker, but my wife will take care of me." He laughed and gave Lynn's hand a squeeze across the table. I used to love all the dumb stuff he did, but lately it was embarrassing. Who said things like "city slicker"?

"Well, sir," said Maggie. She shifted her weight from

one leg to another. "We're very careful here. Horses are gentle animals for the most part, but I've been riding going on forty years, and believe you me, I have a healthy respect for them."

"My husband and I will be happy with the intermediate trail ride," said Lynn, nodding. "Diana and Stephanie probably want to trot or canter some. Is that right, girls?"

"Gallop!" said Diana.

My insides turned watery.

"Well, we have one trail ride for the young people, and what we do while we're out there pretty much depends on the experience level of who we've got."

"Diana, you'll watch out for Stephanie, won't you?" Daddy said.

Now he was asking Diana to babysit me!

"Do I have a choice?" Diana looked like she was getting ready to barf. I saw Lynn point at her temple and tap two times. Diana looked away really fast.

Just then Nick came in the dining room with his parents. Finally! The minute he saw me he waved, and just like that, he brought his mama and daddy over. He'd changed into a polo shirt. It was so cute the way he tried to slick down his hair for supper. He was smilin' again, like he thought just about everything was something to smile about.

"Nick and I met playing horseshoes today," I explained to Daddy.

"Will you folks be riding tomorrow?" Maggie asked as they got settled.

Nick's mama and daddy signed up for the same ride as Lynn and Daddy. Nick would be with Diana and me. I breathed a sigh of relief. With Nick along, even if Diana was mean, I could still have fun. And maybe the trail ride would be nice and slow.

Our waiter brought us barbecued ribs made with the ranch's special sauce, corn on the cob, and butter beans. He came back with baskets of homemade biscuits and plates with mounds of butter that looked like little beehives.

"Everyone should stick around after dinner for a little welcome speech," the waiter said. "They need to get head counts on who's going to Cherokee, and who's going white-water rafting. And then there's housekeeping stuff, like how to keep the garbage away from the raccoons and bears, ranch rules, and so on."

"Bears?" Daddy said. "You're not serious."

"Yessir." Our waiter gave us a grin as he headed over to the next table.

Our parents introduced themselves as they passed the platters.

"I'm Charlene Hansford and this is my husband

Ray," said Nick's mother. "Nick is so glad there are other kids his age here. He'll be in eighth grade."

"So will our girls!" Lynn said.

"We have zero in common," said Diana, and then she laughed really loudly. The conversation came to a complete halt. All the grown-ups stared at her. I felt my face getting hot again.

"You two have lots in common," Lynn said, and she gave Diana a look. She did that tapping thing again on her temple, then reached across the table and patted my hand.

I gave a ghost of a smile. Whoa, this was embarrassing. I could hardly look at Nick.

"I'm Norm Verra and this is Lynn, my bride," Daddy said smoothly. "We got married just last month."

"Congratulations," said Nick's mom.

"You're Stephanie's dad, right?" said Nick. "You look alike."

"That's right." Daddy grinned. "Stephanie and Diana are both awfully lucky to have gotten a new sister out of the deal. Isn't that right, Steph?" Daddy put his arm around me and squeezed my shoulder.

I smiled, then looked down, made sure my napkin was folded in my lap the way Mama taught me.

Right, Daddy.

5

DIANA

Ugh! Stephanie had already met a guy! What a preppie, with those khaki shorts and yellow polo shirt and slick blonde hair. Not my type. Though I hadn't exactly zeroed in on "my type," since most boys acted like I had leprosy. But I could tell this guy Nick liked Stephanie. He kept watching her and smiling and making lame jokes. It was as bad as Norm around Mom.

As soon as the parents said the kids could be excused, Stephanie said, "Y'all want to play horseshoes?"

I said, "Nah," but Nick gave this stupid-looking grin and said, "Sure!"

His dad said, "Go ahead, have fun," and Nick and Stephanie jumped up from the table and practically ran out the door.

Stuck with the grown-ups. Talk about feeling like a complete idiot. Now Mom would say, "Diana, why don't you go play with them?" And I'd try to ignore her, and then she'd say something else, like, "Go ahead, sweetie, you'll have a good time." And then I'd say, "Leave me alone," and go straight to the barn. And then, in just a few minutes, maybe Mom would come down and find me to make sure I was okay.

On cue, Mom said, "Diana, why don't you go play?"

"Only two people can play horseshoes at once, in case you haven't noticed."

"You can switch off. They want you to play, I know they do."

"Hurry up," Norm added. "They're probably starting the game already."

"Go ahead, honey. You'll have fun."

I pushed my chair back from the table and flung open the screen door leading outside. When I turned the corner I saw Nick and Stephanie by the horseshoe pit, laughing and poking each other.

Through the window, I watched Norm move into *my*

empty seat. Put his arm around Mom, obviously telling some lame story. Everyone was laughing. Mom looked like someone in a Happy Meal commercial.

I raced down the road toward the barn. The sun dropped lower. Red and purple started to leak across the horizon like watercolors bleeding across a sheet of paper. A cool, damp breeze tickled the hairs on my arms, and I rubbed my hands over them.

How the heck had Stephanie gotten to know Nick so quick? Geez, we'd only been here a few hours.

Last month, after Mom and Norm got back from their honeymoon, Stephanie came and stayed with us for a weekend. Saturday night I walked in the computer room and Stephanie was online with about thirty people at one time. Boxes popping all over Stephanie's screen with those little sparkling tones that made you feel oh so popular and cool.

"Sup?"

"Hey girl!"

How many little cyberfriends did Stephanie have, anyway? I had looked over her shoulder.

"What's 'lylas'?" I asked.

"'Love you like a sister.' It's just something my friends and I do—that's all." Stephanie didn't look at me.

"Must be southern. Never heard of it." I ended up

spending most of the weekend of Stephanie's visit at the barn. And that's exactly what I'd do this week, too.

The fence gate was locked. I vaulted over. Sprinted across the hard-packed stable yard. The barn door squeaked when I pulled it open. A faint light glowed inside. I felt in my pocket for the carrots and tiptoed across the dirt and straw floor. Copper was probably still awake.

Josie, who managed the barn where I rode, said horses only slept a few hours a night and they only actually laid down for a few minutes. Usually they dozed on their feet with their knees locked. Except for Seabiscuit, the famous racehorse, of course. Seabiscuit used to lie right down in his stall and could sleep through anything.

The rustle of straw came from one of the back stalls. I froze. And listened. But then I didn't hear anything else, so I headed down the center walkway to Copper's stall.

He nickered and poked his beautiful head over the gate as I came up. Wow, he knew me already. I reached up and stroked his jaw and neck, then laughed when he nuzzled my underarm. He must have smelled the carrots.

"Oh, you think I've got something for you, huh? You think so?"

What if Copper could be my own horse? How much

would it cost to buy him? Maybe about a thousand dollars. I'd saved two hundred.

"Hey, the barn's closed."

The sharp voice behind me made me drop Copper's carrot. I whirled around and in the dim light saw a black-haired boy carrying a bucket of water.

"I just came to give Copper a treat," I said and bent to pick up the carrot lying in the dirt.

"Didn't they tell you not to feed the horses at night?"

"I don't know." I did kind of remember that being in the "Welcome to Blah Blah Blah" speech, but so what?

"Well, you're not supposed to feed them." The boy stepped forward and the bare yellow lightbulb outside the office illuminated his sharp cheekbones.

"I'm not hurting anything!" I heard my own voice go higher.

"Yes, you are. They're on special diets. You're not even supposed to be in here." His jeans and T-shirt were both smeared with dirt. His bare forearms were dark and wiry. "Didn't you hear them say no one was allowed in the barn at night?"

Maybe I had heard that. "What's the big deal?"

"Hey, what's with your attitude? It is a big deal." His dark eyebrows swooped downward. His voice got louder.

Copper jerked his head away and disappeared into the back of his stall.

My shrink's voice sneaked into my head. *"Take a breath. Focus. Think about what you're going to say before you say it. Admit it if you've been wrong."*

Moronic Mood-o-Meter hovering at six point five.

I took a breath. "I'm sorry. I came in here because I, well, I … fell in love with Copper."

The boy's face got softer. "I'm just trying to help Maggie out," he said. "She's my grandmother."

I searched the boy's face and something about his eyes did look like Maggie's. "Really? She seems so cool. I can't wait to ride with her."

The boy's face opened a little more. "She put me on a horse the first time when I was three years old."

"Wow." This boy was probably an incredible rider. I'd love to go riding with him and Maggie. I didn't want him mad at me. "I'm sorry I didn't pay attention."

"It's okay." He shrugged, but he kept his eyes on my face. "I like hanging out in the barn myself."

Suddenly I felt self-conscious. I felt heat on my neck and cheeks.

And then one of the eeriest, most lonesome animal sounds I'd ever heard started out low and sad and arced through the air for so long it made the hair on my arms and neck stand on end.

The boy heard it, too. The spell was broken. He grabbed the water bucket and hung it on the hook by the sink. "I've got to go, and you've got to leave."

"What was that?"

He practically herded me out of the barn. His fingers grazed my back very lightly.

"Was that a wolf?" I said.

"Yeah," he said. "A wolf that's not being allowed to be a wolf."

"What do you mean?" The boy and I were outside the barn now. He closed the tall wooden door.

"Nothing," he said. "I gotta go." He climbed over the fence and then straddled a four-wheeler parked outside the gate. He turned the key and it roared to life, shattering the quiet mountain night. He sped off down the dirt road.

A wolf that was not being allowed to be a wolf. What did that mean?

The shadows stretched long and dark as I headed for the lodge. I was shivering now. I'd thought maybe Mom would be out on the grounds outside the lodge looking for me. But yellow light spilled from the dining room window. Mom and Norm still sat at the long wood table across from the Hansfords, laughing, Norm's arm over Mom's shoulders. A bottle of wine on the table between them. Outside under the tree in a circle of light, Stephanie and Nick still threw horseshoes. The sound of their laughter seemed to travel farther in the dark. Everyone was enveloped in the warmth of the laughter and golden lights. Except me.

And that lonesome wolf.

6

STEPHANIE

I started getting better at horseshoes. I finally beat Nick once.

"Pay up, buddy-ro!" I said, giving his arm a light smack.

"Hey, I didn't know we were betting. How come we weren't betting all the times I won?"

"I changed the rules." I started giggling.

"Just like a girl. Change the rules on me." Nick sat on the picnic table. "So, your dad and stepmom just got married a month ago? Is that weird or what?"

I shrugged. "Not everybody can say they got to be a junior bridesmaid twice in one year."

"Do I detect a note of sarcasm?"

"No, really," I said. "At my mama's wedding we got to ride in a horse and carriage. And in the front hall at the country club there was a swan four feet tall that was made out of ice. And there were huge strawberries that were decorated with chocolate. It was so funny— the strawberries looked like they were wearing little tuxedos. And Daddy's wedding was like a backyard thing. Daddy just wore a nice suit and Lynn wore a tea-length dress. But it was still real nice." I could tell Nick was getting kind of bored, so I changed the subject. "*And* now I'm going to have two bedrooms. And I have a stepbrother who's a freshman in college."

"That would be cool. What about the stepsister that's here, what's her name? Diana? You get along?"

"Sure." I picked at a string on my jeans.

Nick's mama and daddy came out of the dining room. It had gotten pretty dark, and I could barely see them. "Nick!" His mama called. "We're heading back to the cabin."

"I'll be there in a few minutes," he called back.

"All right, don't be too long."

I could see the whites of Nick's eyes as he rolled them in my direction.

"Such protective parental units," I whispered, smiling.

"When you're an only child, it's like they're focused on you like a laser beam, you know."

"Yep," I said. "I know." I could tell he liked me.

* * *

Later that night, I couldn't sleep, and I stared through the shadows at the lump in the next bed that was Diana. She'd barely said a word to me all night. I'd been right in the middle of telling her a story about playing horseshoes with Nick, and she'd crawled into bed and switched off the bedside lamp. If Diana was a normal person, that would have really hurt my feelings.

At youth group, my teacher, Aunt Lana, had led a discussion once about what God would want us to do in certain relationships. We had actually talked about the movie *Toy Story*, about how Woody never gave up on friendship. We had talked about when it was time to give up on someone, and Aunt Lana had said, with God, the time is "never." God never gives up.

So, I need to keep trying with Diana. Daddy would want me to keep trying. I shouldn't give up, even if she doesn't respond yet.

I wish I could talk to her about the horses. One of

them had stared at me today. Its big brown eye had a white rim around the edge that made it look wild, kind of out of its mind. It had a thin stream of snot running out of its nostril, and flies kept buzzing around. What if my horse reared tomorrow, like the one three years ago? What if I fell off again? I hoped Maggie gave me the oldest, most decrepit horse in the barn. I didn't care if I rode a horse that could hardly walk.

I couldn't fake being sick. Mama fell for that sometimes but Daddy never did. He would make me go. Daddy was always saying stuff like he did at supper tonight. Tough it out, sport. I turned over my pillow and pulled the covers up over my shoulders.

DIANA

I climbed the split rail fence, swung my leg over the top, and watched the wranglers bring out the horses. I'd eaten about two bites of breakfast, grabbed my riding helmet, and then raced down to the barn. Halfway down here, I realized I'd forgotten my pill, but there was no way I was going back. Besides, it would make me feel all fuzzy again.

The Appaloosa came out first, with his giant white legs and long silky tail. Maggie would ride him.

They brought out a frisky quarter horse and a Palomino mare. The mare shoved past the quarter horse, and I could tell that she was ahead of the quarter horse in the pecking order.

I loved finding out about the pecking order in every barn. Who was the alpha, the number one mare? Who was the beta, or the number two? Who was the omega, the lowest in the pecking order? I loved finding out which horses were friends. Most barns had two that had to stay together because they were best buddies. Like Seabiscuit. Here he was, this moody racehorse who half the time didn't even feel like running. Then they found him a steady little pony to be his buddy, and they stayed together in the same stall until Seabiscuit died. That was so sweet. I loved that story.

And usually there would be another two horses you couldn't put together because they hated each other's guts. Usually there was one mare, probably brought in from another barn, who hated all the other horses, and the other horses would hate her. Once Josie, our barn manager, told me that having a barn full of horses was like having a classroom full of kindergartners.

Maggie, wearing her floppy hat, led Copper out. There he was! His legs weren't exactly spindly; they were delicate. And his head was small and chiseled. Definitely had some Arabian in him. Copper shifted his weight, tossed his mane, and switched his tail. He'd canter and maybe even gallop easily. I jumped down from the fence and hurried over. I felt in my pocket for one of the carrots I'd stolen at dinner last night.

"You said I could ride him, right? Can I?" I begged Maggie.

"He's a mite high-strung," said Maggie, as she checked his saddle and stirrups. "But if he trusts you and he knows you're boss, you'll do fine. Just wait by the fence while we finish bringing out the rest of the horses."

"Can I give him a carrot?"

"Well, he's already got the bit in his mouth. Here, give him a sugar cube." Maggie handed me one from the pocket of her jeans.

"Hey, Copper, c'mere, I brought a treat for you."

I could feel Maggie watching as I held my flattened palm under Copper's velvety lips. He gobbled the sugar cube. Butted my shoulder for another one.

"When Copper butts you that means he likes you," said Maggie. "That's good." She moved away.

I leaned close. Rubbed my hands over the smooth dark fur on Copper's head and neck. He watched me from under thick, angled lashes at least three inches long. Oh, man, he was so beautiful.

"Is he for sale?" I asked.

"Shoot, no," Maggie snorted. "We just got 'im."

Foamy slobber dripped from the metal edges of Copper's bit as he finished the sugar cube.

"Oooh, gross!" Stephanie stood by the fence, leaning up against Mom. Held one hand over her mouth as she watched the string of slobber stretch from Copper's mouth to the ground. She was wearing her little rhinestone-studded blue jeans. She looked like she was getting ready to go audition for the country music station or something.

Norm hadn't even come down from the lodge yet.

"Okay, the trail ride for the young people will be saddling up and leaving in about five minutes. Everybody go to the tack room and find a helmet." Maggie pointed to the doorway just inside the barn.

"I brought my own helmet," I showed how I'd threaded the chin strap through one of the belt loops of my jeans.

"Well, put it on," Maggie said. She didn't seem as impressed as I had hoped.

Stephanie ducked into the tack room with Nick. What a prepster. They were laughing and acting like they'd known each other a million years.

"Have other people worn these helmets?" Stephanie asked one of the wranglers. "Don't you wash them or anything?" She held the round black helmet out in front of her but didn't put it on.

"We spray 'em," said the wrangler.

"Yuck."

"You have to wear it," said Maggie. "Ranch rules."

I laughed and reached up to scratch Copper's ears.

"Oh, I forgot to tell you," said Maggie, as she led out a sleepy gray mare. "Be careful—he's head shy."

I didn't answer. Instead, I calmly rubbed my palms over Copper's nose, forehead, ears, poll, crest, and neck. He never flinched. I could tell Maggie was impressed.

Ten minutes later everyone was mounted. I got right on and sat stroking Copper's neck. Laughed to myself as I watched the rest of them slide down the saddles, get their boots twisted in the stirrups, and fall over the horses' withers, which is sort of like their shoulder. Ballou, the mare Stephanie was supposed to ride, actually started walking away while Stephanie was trying to get on her. Maggie had to yell at Ballou and smack her on the rump. Nick was on Silver, the quarter horse, getting his stirrups adjusted. There were two younger girls, who looked about eight, on small geldings with droopy heads and knock-knees who looked like they barely had the gumption to walk fast. I seriously hoped they were going on a different trail ride.

"What's your horse's name?" I asked Maggie.

"Chief Tenkiller," said Maggie.

"Is he mean?" asked Stephanie.

"Oh, he wouldn't hurt a fly," Maggie said, leaning back to give his rump an affectionate smack with the flat of her hand. A small cloud of dust and horsehair flew up.

"Can I go right behind you?" asked Stephanie. Her laugh sounded really nervous.

"No, I've got to put these two younger girls behind me," said Maggie. "You can be third, then Copper, then Silver."

This was looking less and less like an exciting trail ride.

"Can we gallop?" I called with one last shred of hope as we headed out of the barnyard and up the trail.

"Afraid not," said Maggie, turning in her saddle and tipping her floppy hat. "Too many inexperienced riders today."

Oh, man. This is going to be the most boring trail ride ever to take place on planet Earth.

We headed up a dirt road beside a slanted mountain pasture dotted with white salt chunks and tiny yellow flowers. Horses grazing in the pasture looked up to watch us go by. The sky stretched above, a cool blue with wispy clouds.

Still at a walk, we wound upward from the pasture to a woodland path. Copper placed his small hooves carefully on the trail, avoiding roots and rocks. He tried to eat some leaves from an overhanging tree branch, but I said, "Not now, buddy," and he pulled his head away. Maggie led us at the speed of a slug, telling these stories about the Cherokee Indians who used to live around there. Blah blah blah. Stephanie's horse, Ballou, was lazy, lagging behind, leaving lots of space between him and the two geldings ahead. Copper wanted to go faster. His muzzle was inches from Ballou's tail. I knew I should hold him back. But it was just all so boring!

Copper's withers pulled even with Ballou's flank.

I saw it happening. Ballou swung her head sideways at Copper. Showed the white of her eye and pinned back her ears. A second later, she kicked. Copper reared. I grabbed my reins and kept my seat with no trouble, but Stephanie screamed, and then Ballou broke into a trot.

Stephanie started sliding off. In a minute she'd fall. She was crying like a baby.

Well, I didn't think it would go that far. I dug my heels into Copper's sides, cantered up alongside, and grabbed Ballou's reins, pulling her back to a walk.

Stephanie was shaking.

"Get yourself back up in the saddle, Stephanie," I said. "I've got the reins; she's not going anywhere." Somehow I managed to lean over and help her back up on top of the horse.

Maggie was watching from farther up the trail. She couldn't come back to help us because of the two younger kids in between. "Can you keep riding, or do you want to go back?" she called.

Stephanie pushed the hair that had slipped from her braid off her wet face. "Go back."

Maggie looked at me. "Can you take your sister back to the barn?"

Excuse me, Stephanie's not my sister, and no, I don't want to take her back to the barn, I started to say. Then I thought about it: once I got Stephanie back to the barn, I could go back out on my own. Just me and Copper.

"Sure, no problem," I said. I dismounted. Held Ballou and Copper's reins while Nick passed us on the path.

"Hope you're okay." Nick said to Stephanie as he rode by on Silver. He looked *so* concerned. Oh, *please.* "Hey," he said. "I don't mind taking her back if you want to keep on riding."

"No, no, I promised the 'rents I'd take care of her," I said, giving him a really sweet smile. "I better do it myself." I turned both horses around and remounted, using Ballou's reins as a lead. "Hold on to the saddle horn," I told Stephanie, as we headed back down the trail. "I thought you took lessons."

"I did." Stephanie heaved this big shaky sigh. "Thanks for taking me back."

"It's okay," I said. That was amazing. Stephanie had no idea that I could have kept Copper from spooking Ballou. I would have liked it better if she'd yelled at me.

As one of the barn hands was helping Stephanie dismount, I turned Copper around and left. I mean, she was so pathetic, crying and shaking and stuff. Copper didn't seem too excited about going out now that he'd been back to the barn, but I ignored him and made him go back out on the trail.

He was skittish at first, all confused about what was going on. I leaned forward, clucking to him. Got him into a smooth rolling canter on the wide, flat trail beside the pasture. The wind crossed my face and my hair bounced on my shoulders in rhythm with his rocking gait. His hooves pounded the earth like a heartbeat. I had no plans to catch the others at all. I could ride by myself all day.

I ended up on a trail I'd seen on the way out, a narrow, dark path leading farther up the mountain and deeper into the woods. I was hoping it would open up into one of those high mountain meadows where I could get Copper to gallop. But now I slowed him to a walk, telling him what a good job he'd done. His neck, when I slid my palm over it, felt smooth and solid. His hooves made hollow sounds on the occasional rock, and he flicked his ears when birds darted through the shadows across the trail. I let my backbone relax. Settled more deeply into Copper's gait. We moved almost like one living thing now, talking to each other with small nudges and pressures.

Suddenly Copper stood stock-still. His ears went back. The crest of his dark mane rose.

"What is it, boy?" I leaned forward, soothing him. I stroked his neck. His shoulder muscles bunched up under my legs. He stepped sideways, tossed his head, gave a nervous snort. My heart tripped and tightened.

And that was when I saw the wolf. Big wide paws planted on a high rock. Bushy fur covered its ears, head, and back like a gray hooded cape clasped at the neck. Peeking from beneath the cape of gray were an ivory snout and throat, a round black nose. Topaz black-rimmed eyes trained on me like lasers.

I locked eyes with the wolf for only an instant, but in that instant I felt a bizarre shock of recognition. I could feel Copper fidgeting, but I was frozen, not the least bit afraid. What passed between me and the wolf was like a bizarre beam of energy. I felt as if I was peering into the wolf's soul, and the wolf was peering into mine. I stared until my eyelids burned. Finally, with the tiniest flick of its eyes, the wolf glanced away.

With extreme relief, I blinked. For the first time, I saw that between me and the wolf was a chain-link fence about ten feet high. A black and red sign said **DANGER: HIGH VOLTAGE**. The wolf was in a pen about the size of the dining room at the lodge. Behind the rock, the ground was bare and dusty. Two empty metal bowls were overturned, and there were some yellowing bushes and a couple of trees with the bark rubbed off. I smelled the wolf now—sharp and musky. I scanned the pen and saw a shadow behind one of the bushes that might be another wolf. Probably two of the most miserable looking creatures I'd ever seen.

8

STEPHANIE

I ran away from the barn, wiping my face dry with the end of my T-shirt. I probably had mascara all over my face. My shirt and jeans had dirt all over them and somehow I had to get home and shower. Everybody was still out on the trail. I followed the path toward the lodge. I couldn't quit crying. I didn't know where to go. Daddy was going to be so mad at me.

My knees were all wobbly, and when I breathed in, my insides shook, too. As hard as I tried, I couldn't stop the tears from squeezing out my eyes and roll-ing down my cheeks. A light-colored horse in a pen beside the barn walked over as I passed, poking its big old head over the fence. I moved to the other side of the path and kept on walking. That horse followed me with these great big eyes.

I kept having this memory of galloping down that path, almost falling off the horse, and tree limbs scratching my face. I saw myself, over and over again, falling and trying to hold on to the reins, and some-thing in my shoulder kind of making this crunching noise, like before. That time, when they helped me up, my shoulder was at this funny angle. It hurt so much when the doctor had to push it back into place. I just hate it that I get so scared about this.

There was no way to keep Daddy from finding out. Maggie was bound to tell him. At least Diana had been nice enough to bring me back. I couldn't believe Nick had seen that whole thing. He must have thought I was the world's biggest baby.

I wished Mama was here. She wouldn't have made me ride.

I about died when I saw Nick's parents heading down the steps from the lodge. If they saw me crying, I'd be embarrassed to death. I ducked down a fork in the path with a little wooden sign that said "To the

Pond." By the time I realized that the path led right into the woods, it was too late. I glanced back, and Nick's parents were still standing there looking at the big wooden ranch map, so I just gritted my teeth and kept right on going. I saw flicks of water through the trees, kind of flashing like mica in a rock, so maybe the pond wasn't far. I walked through shadowy places and then into patches of sun where those sweet little pink flowers bloomed.

The path wound deeper into the quiet of the woods. Cool air raised chill bumps on my arms. The only sounds were my own footsteps, muffled by the pine needles. Crawling sensations on my face made me think I'd walked through a cobweb. I was about to turn back when suddenly the pond was right in front of me. I heard gurgling somewhere near the other end and figured that was the stream that fed the pond. The water was dark, almost black, and the surface was like a mirror reflecting the trees along its banks. I knelt down and touched the water with my fingertips. Freezing!

The reflections reminded me of something Maggie had said on our trail ride about the Cherokee Indians. They believe every person, animal, river, and rock in the world is a reflection of a star in the sky. And they call the Milky Way "The Path of Souls." Maggie had said that souls enter the path by Sirius, the Dog Star.

They leave by the star Antares, the Great Mother Wolf. Souls can get trapped in the Milky Way if the spirits don't like them.

I sat down under a tree, took a deep breath, and stared at the still surface of the water. What was under there? It looked so dark. Today I'd felt trapped by being so afraid. Cool air from the pond kind of swirled across my arms. I got up and hurried out of the woods, hugging myself and staring at the long shifting shadows behind every tree. My riding boots hurt. Daddy had given me a key to the condo. I'd go back and take the boots off. Get the barn dirt and cobwebs off. Wash my hair.

The door to the condo was unlocked when I got back, and I headed upstairs to the loft. I pulled my new boots off over big old leaky blisters on both heels. Diana's were beat-up, but at that minute I realized she probably didn't have a single blister. I lined up my shower gel, shampoo, and conditioner on the bathroom counter, took a deep breath, and got in the shower.

The water pummeled my body, streamed through my hair, and made me feel more relaxed. Just as I was getting out, I heard Daddy's voice downstairs. I held perfectly still, not breathing. If Daddy found out I was here, he'd know that something happened on the trail ride.

"Do you think Stephanie was okay riding today, Norm?" Lynn was saying. "I think she was pretty nervous."

I stood as still as a mouse, holding my breath.

"Well, maybe she was. She's always been kind of a scaredy-cat, Lynn, and I really want to get her out of that."

"It's hard, though, if you're scared. You can't just ignore the fear."

I heard somebody open the refrigerator, then a cabinet door shut. "I think she just needs to get control of herself."

I felt dizzy.

Something inside me was shrinking. I was shrinking. I felt smaller and smaller.

"I don't think it's that easy, Norm. Fears can be hard to overcome. We've all got them."

"Stephanie's a pretty girl; she's got a great little personality; good grief, she's so smart. Never less than an 'A' in school. She gets along well with everyone; the girl's got it all. I'm trying to understand why she's so afraid of everything, but it's hard. Part of me wants to say, 'Suck it up, kiddo, this is life.'"

My stomach started to hurt really bad. I took two Tums.

DIANA

At dinner I could barely eat anything. I had to get back to see those wolves. I wouldn't take Copper again, in case he got spooked. Maybe I'd take one of those bikes I'd seen in front of the lodge. Maybe even after dinner.

Maggie came over to our table, still in her riding stuff. "Did Stephanie tell you what happened during the trail ride this morning?" she asked.

"No, what happened?" asked Norm. Stephanie, sitting

across the table next to Nick, ducked her head when her dad looked at her. I looked away before Mom could catch my eye.

"She had a bit of trouble," said Maggie. "I'd like her to spend some time at the barn, helping out with the horses, to get more comfortable around them before she rides again. How does that sound, Stephanie?"

Stephanie looked up from her lap. "Do I have to?"

"If you want to ride again, I think you should."

"I don't have to ride again."

"If you don't want to, then," Mom started to say, but Norm interrupted.

"Sure you do," he said. He reached across the table and patted Stephanie's hand. She yanked her hand away. Maggie shrugged. "Well, come by the barn tomorrow morning." She looked at me. "And now you."

I sucked in my breath. Now Maggie was probably going to yell at me for dumping Stephanie at the barn. Taking Copper out alone. Right in front of Mom and Norm.

"Thanks for taking Stephanie back to the barn today. And you did a nice job of putting Copper's tack away. Since you missed most of the trail ride, would you like to come out tomorrow morning with my advanced group? We're leaving early—about six thirty or seven."

I met Maggie's eyes. The comment about putting the

tack away meant Maggie knew exactly how long I'd stayed on the trail by myself. She knew everything. Maybe even that I purposely hadn't held Copper back when he moved up beside Stephanie's pony. But she'd decided not to tell Mom and Norm.

"Sure," I said, flashing Maggie a grin. "Can I ride Copper again?"

Maggie nodded. "Seems like you two clicked pretty good." Then she went to the fireplace. Clapped her hands to get everyone's attention. "After dinner, those who are interested come on out on the back porch. You'll get to meet some wolves."

I sat up straight. Wolves? Suddenly everything fell into place. The ones I'd seen today were the wolves Maggie was talking about. And that's why Maggie had taken the meat from the kitchen. That's why that boy had chased me out of the barn. All afternoon I'd been haunted by that wolf's yellow eyes.

"Diana, aren't you going to finish your ice cream?" Mom asked.

My sundae had turned to creamy soup in the bowl. "No, I'm full. I'm going out to see the wolves."

I hurried to the back porch and grabbed what I hoped was the best seat at one of the outdoor picnic tables.

Stephanie came outside with Nick and sat beside me.

"Have you ever seen a wolf?" Nick asked Stephanie.

"I saw one today," I said. They both stopped staring at each other for two seconds and stared at me instead.

"No way," Nick said.

A kind of mean-looking man wearing a camouflage jacket and a salt-and-pepper beard came onto the porch. He glanced at us but didn't smile or say hello. "Hurry up," he said to someone behind him. "Bring them on the porch and wait here." He went inside the lodge.

And then who should come onto the porch but the boy from the barn. And right behind him, coming out of the shadows, were two long snouts, yellow black-rimmed eyes, and powerful rippling shoulders. With long, rangy legs and paws twice the size of a dog's, the two wolves were on leashes. It didn't seem right. They had a strong, musky smell, like a forest during a rain storm, or damp earth covered with autumn leaves. A wild animal smell.

One of the wolves was so scared it was crawling on its belly. I could hardly stand to look.

The other wolf was the one I'd seen on the rock. It was bolder, but still walked with its haunches low to the ground, ready to bolt at any moment. I memorized its hooded head, its searing yellow eyes, its triangular gray ears. It paced back and forth, watching, listening, smelling. Its eyes, ears, and nose seemed many times keener than any human's. Would the wolf remember me?

"Hey." The boy flashed even, white teeth in a smile. He had straight dark hair that was a little longer than most boys wore it. He wore old jeans and a faded flannel shirt. "We met down at the barn, right? My name's Russell."

"Diana," I muttered, feeling the strange heat flush my neck again.

"Any of you folks want to pet Waya?" he asked.

Stephanie shook her head, and so did Nick. I liked the way Russell's hand rested on the wolf's head, relaxed and gentle.

"Could I?" I asked.

Russell nodded. "Go ahead." Russell had one chain link leash curled around each brown wrist. As I approached, the timid wolf slid along the floor behind Russell's leg. The bolder wolf stopped her pacing and stared at me. Slowly, I reached out and let my fingertips brush the top of Waya's head. She watched me with unwavering yellow eyes. Braver now, I ran my whole palm across her head and down the back of her neck. Her fur was coarser than a dog's, stiff and thick. She didn't move, just watched me with those yellow wolf eyes. She seemed to look through me. Then, she lowered her snout toward my hand. I stopped breathing. I stared into her eyes, wondering if I'd made a mistake. The cool wet of her nose barely touched my hand.

I looked up from the wolf to Russell.

"Good girl, Waya," Russell said. Looking away from me, he added, "She likes you." He stood up. Cleared his throat. "Okay, everyone find somewhere to sit." I sat down again, practically shaking with excitement. A damp layer of oil or dirt from the stiff bristles of Waya's fur coated my palm, and my hand smelled like wild animal. All the children sat or knelt in a semicircle, with the adults gathered behind them.

"I'm Russell Morgan. My dad is the owner of these wolf dogs."

I was surprised that the grumpy-looking man was Russell's father.

"This is Waya, which means 'wolf' in Cherokee." Russell knelt and stroked Waya's head and back. "And this timid one is Oginali, which is Cherokee for 'friend.' We're in western North Carolina, which is the homeland of the eastern band of the Cherokee Indians, and the Cherokee have special reverence for wolves." Russell crouched. He tried to comfort Oginali. Then he stood and held the chain leash tight as Waya paced the edge of the circle of curious people. "Waya and Oginali here are ninety-eight percent wolf. My dad got them from a Cherokee woman who breeds wolves with dogs. It's against the law to keep a full-blooded wolf as a pet."

Waya paced, back and forth, back and forth. Oginali

cowered behind Russell's leg. I had never seen an animal so afraid.

"Wolves used to roam all over these Smoky Mountains, but now they're extinct," Russell said. "People have hunted down and killed every one of them. For some reason, people are scared to death of wolves. My dad keeps them because he believes they're misunderstood." Russell reached down to stroke Oginali's head, as if he knew what that meant. I loved the gentle way he treated her.

Misunderstood? I met Waya's eyes again. I knew a little about that.

Russell went on. "There's been people trying to bring back the red wolf over in the eastern part of the state. But people are scared. They say wolves kill their livestock. They're afraid they'll kill people. But do you know how many people have been killed by healthy wolves in the US? Just guess."

Russell hesitated, waiting for someone to answer. One person said, "A hundred."

"No. Zero." Russell held up his fingers to form a round zero. "None. Wolves are shy animals. They stay away from people if they can."

Russell held up the thick chain that circled Waya's neck. "If your dog runs away, he'll get hungry and come back. But Waya here is ninety-eight percent wild animal. If she was freed for only one second, she'd be gone forever."

I quickly raised my hand. "Where do you keep the wolves?"

"In a pen," Russell said. "Dad made the fence ten feet high so they can't escape."

I remembered the dusty ground, the empty over- turned bowls. A wolf could starve to death in a pen like that. I had a vision of Waya disappearing into the shadows with a single bound. Waya would like that, wouldn't she? To be free?

Someone asked what the wolves ate.

Russell pulled the sleeve of his shirt down over his hand and held it out stiffly. "People's hands!" He grinned. "Kidding!" He popped his hand back out. "Waya and Oginali, they eat anything. Dog food. Meat. Cameras. Buckets. Fishing poles. Tents."

People were laughing now.

"Me and Maggie, my grandma, sometimes drive around in a pickup and collect road kill to feed 'em."

Behind me, Stephanie groaned. I grinned at Russell. Gross-out stuff didn't bother me. He caught my eye and grinned back, pulled a bowl from his backpack, and placed dry dog food out for the wolves to eat.

Oginali hung back, waiting for Waya to eat first. Waya scanned the crowd and the darkness, cocking her ears, then tentatively lowered her head and ate. When Waya was finished she walked away from the dish. Oginali took two steps forward, practically crawling on the ground, then slunk back under the chair. Russell said that often Waya ate all the food, even if she wasn't hungry, just so Oginali wouldn't get any. Sometimes she would even pee on the food to keep Oginali from eating it.

"Why is Waya so mean to Oginali?" I recognized Stephanie's voice coming from behind me.

"That's the way wolf packs work. Waya is the alpha wolf, or dominant wolf, and Oginali is the omega. Every pack has an alpha and omega. The omega is the one who gets picked on. But Oginali gets something out of this, too. The alpha is always in charge of the safety of the pack. So Waya keeps watch, fights if she has to, to keep Oginali safe. Oginali doesn't have to worry. That's their deal."

The wolf pack and the horse herd are not that different, I thought. Watching the two wolves, I wondered, Didn't Oginali hate Waya for eating all her food? And didn't Waya hate Oginali for always needing her protection?

"The most important thing in a wolf's life is the pack," said Russell. "You might think Waya is mean to Oginali, and if they were released, Oginali would want to get as far away from Waya as she could. But if I let these wolves go, they'd most likely stay together. Oginali would probably follow Waya."

I stared at the two wolves. How could that be?

Russell was talking to Oginali now in a soft voice, the same kind of voice I used to talk to Copper. I liked listening to his voice.

"No more questions?" The mean tone of Russell's dad's voice made me jump. He turned to Maggie. "Who has my check?"

Mr. Morgan was getting paid for showing us the wolves? That seemed wrong, as if Waya and Oginali were circus animals or something. I could tell Maggie didn't like it, either. Or maybe it was just Mr. Morgan she didn't like.

"Check with Warren in the office," Maggie turned her back.

A few kids wanted to go over to pet Waya. No one petted Oginali because she had backed under a chair. I hung around, waiting for the rest to leave. After the last kid ran off, I sat on a picnic bench beside Waya, and I held out my palm again.

"Russell," said his dad. "Put the wolves back in the truck."

Russell stared at his dad, but didn't do anything right away.

"What does it mean if a wolf likes you?" I asked Russell.

Russell picked up the food bowls. "I guess it means the wolf trusts you not to hurt it."

I stroked Waya's head, studied her golden eyes. "I would never hurt her. Never in a million years."

"I wish my dad felt that way," Russell muttered. "Hang on to her while I get Oginali," Russell handed me Waya's leash, then knelt and tried coaxing Oginali out from under the chair.

I held the leash while Waya paced back and forth, keeping her eyes on Russell. I noticed a shiny pink scar on Waya's nose. Waya's chain collar was buried deeply in her fur. I slid my fingers down behind the collar to see if it was too tight. No one was looking. I loosened it one notch.

During the presentation, Russell had said that a wild wolf's territory was about forty miles. But Waya lived in that pen.

I looked at the leash wrapped around my hand. All I had to do was just let it go, just like that. Waya would be free.

Russell straightened up as Oginali crawled out from under the chair. "Thanks a lot," he said. "You're good with her. It's like you and Waya have a kind of thing going. Want to help me put her back in the truck?"

"Sure," I said. I wrapped the leash around my hand once more.

"We have to put Waya in first," Russell said as we crossed the dark parking lot. "If Oginali gets in first, Waya will attack her."

"That is so weird."

"Last year, there was this guy in seventh grade," Russell said. "No one would sit with him at lunch or on the bus. Everyone said he stunk. People teased him. It's that way with wolves. Males and females, they single out the omega. Maybe she's small like Oginali, but for whatever reason, they just pick and pick."

Waya and Oginali strained on their leashes, tense, half-crouching, as they padded along beside us. Each time one of us spoke, the wolves's ears cocked backwards listening.

"Same at our school," I said. "But it seems like every year, someone different gets harassed." One someone had been me, I thought. I knew what it was like, all right. Mom and Dad's divorce had been terrible in every way but one—and that was getting to move to a new school when Mom had to sell the house. "I got picked on in third grade, the year my folks split up." I'd never talked to anyone about it, and here I was telling Russell. But I'd started and I had to finish. I hesitated. I hid the shaking of my hand by tucking my hair behind my ear. I didn't want to alienate him. "No one would sit with me, either," I said quietly, envisioning our lunchroom. "Or they copied everything I said for the whole lunch period. They smashed my lunch. Stuck chewed gum on my chair. Poured milkshakes in my soccer bag."

"I know what you mean," Russell said softly, like he was talking to Oginali.

The way he said it, I just knew. It had happened to him, too.

"It happened to me in fifth grade. The year Mom died."

"Your mom died?"

"Car wreck."

"Oh! That's terrible. I'm sorry." I felt dizzy.

"Thanks."

The silence stretched between us. Then I said, "Seems like they go after you when you're down."

"Yep." Russell lowered the gate to the back of the truck. Inside were two large dog kennels, side by side. He unlocked both gates. Swung them open.

"Okay," Russell said. "I'll put her in now."

I handed him Waya's leash.

"Let's go, girl," he said. He tossed a dog treat into the back of the kennel. Waya jumped onto the truck bed and walked into the narrow crate. I heard her crunching the dog biscuit. Russell slammed the door behind her. The kennel was just big enough for her to turn around and she did, keeping her eyes on Russell and me. Then he threw a treat for Oginali. She hesitated, looking fearfully up at Waya and then at Russell. Finally, she jumped up and slunk into her kennel. I didn't hear her crunching the dog biscuit.

"She won't eat until she's sure Waya's finished," Russell explained. He slammed the gate of the truck. "Thanks. See ya later."

"Wait … um, could I come visit Waya this week?"

Russell shook his head. "Not a good idea. Dad doesn't like people seeing where he keeps them."

I opened my mouth to tell Russell it was too late for that now, but quickly closed it again. He'd think I was a snoop. I didn't let anything show on my face. Through the wire mesh of the kennel gate, I met Waya's eyes. Again, in my mind, I saw her leaping to freedom. And I wondered, was it possible to exchange thoughts with an animal?

10

STEPHANIE

As darkness fell, the air cooled, and the sky turned deep purple. Nick went to a movie with his folks. He'd wanted to invite me, but his parents said no. It was family time. Daddy had stopped at the front desk to ask about white-water rafting, and Diana was helping Russell put the wolves back in their cages in the truck.

Diana acted all weird with those wolves, like she was obsessed with them or something, asking all those questions and running her hands over that one wolf's head. I can't believe she was touching it like that! Was she crazy?

The path to our cabin was dark and kind of spooky, so I ran to catch up with Lynn. She stopped and waited for me, and when I reached her, she brushed hair from my forehead with her fingertips, real gently, just like Mama did sometimes.

"I wanted to ask you something," Lynn said. "The horses scare you, don't they?"

"Well ... a little."

Lynn slid her arm over my shoulder. "Would you like me to talk to your dad, get him to take the pressure off?" The pine needles on the path were quiet and springy under our feet. The flashlight beam caught a toad the size of an acorn hopping into the damp grass. A cricket chirped.

I took a deep breath. "You'd do that?"

"Sure." We climbed the steps to the cabin, and Lynn fished the key from her back pocket. "I'll talk with him tonight."

"Wow, that would be great." At that very minute I felt really relieved. Then, for some reason, I started to not feel so good about it. It felt like I was giving up. Not the kind of girl Daddy wanted me to be. Not perfect. But then I thought, why should I keep trying to be so perfect for Daddy? He's already disappointed in me, so why bother?

I followed Lynn into the cabin living room. Lynn laid the flashlight on the kitchen counter, switched on a lamp, and headed back to the room she shared with Daddy.

"Hey, want to put on some music?" Lynn went into the bedroom, half-shutting the door. "And maybe we can play a family game when your dad and Diana get back."

"Okay." I lined up the CDs, glancing over when I saw Lynn pass across the half-open door to the bedroom. I used to follow Mama back into her room, lie on the bed, and watch her get ready to go places. Mama let me play with her jeweled glass perfume bottles and try on her lipsticks and blushes. Once, when I was about seven or eight, Mama let me wear her makeup to the grocery store. Daddy had gotten mad about that.

I didn't go in Daddy and Lynn's room now. I didn't think Lynn was a person who wore perfume—I couldn't smell it the way I could with Mama. I knew from just seeing a glimpse now and then that Lynn wore plain white underwear. She wore the same silver hoops in her ears every day, and had only one ring other than the one Daddy had given her. Lynn was a physician's assistant, so she didn't even dress up to go to work. She just wore a white jacket with her name on the pocket.

I put on a mixed CD. Lynn came out wearing a gray sweatshirt just as Daddy came in, carrying a couple of white-water-rafting brochures.

"So?" said Lynn. "What'd you find out?" They spread the brochures on the kitchen counter and sat on the tall stools there. Daddy massaged the back of Lynn's neck. I crawled onto the stool beside Lynn and craned to see the pictures on the brochures of families in yellow rafts, wearing orange life vests and helmets, roaring down a river, screaming their fool heads off.

"Okay, we can go down the Big Pigeon or the Nantahala," Daddy said. "Both of them have class three and four rapids. The Nantahala has one class five. The Nantahala is also much colder, apparently."

"I went down the Nantahala in college and had a blast," said Lynn. "But since you're a city slicker, Norm, we probably ought to do the Big Pigeon. You know, very calm. Sort of like rafting in a warm bathtub. The city slicker river." Lynn raised her eyebrows and smiled at Daddy in a real flirty way.

"I vote for the Big Pigeon," I said. But nobody was paying any attention to me.

"You think I'm too chicken to go down the Nantahala?" Daddy was nose to nose with Lynn, half-smiling. He didn't even look at me, but I started wondering, Is he trying to make it dangerous just to make me suck it up?

"I do," said Lynn. Hooking her thumbs under her arms, she did an imitation of a chicken, flapping her elbows. "Brraak! Brrraaak!"

"Oh, yeah? I happen to be an excellent swimmer. I was a lifeguard in college."

"Some shallow suburban gene pool, right?" Lynn teased. "You sat on a lifeguard stand and twirled a whistle to the right ... then twirled your whistle to the left." Lynn pantomimed whistle twirling. "Norm Verra ... expert whistle twirler."

Lynn pantomimed one last time, and Daddy tickled her ribcage. Lynn screamed and tried to get away. "Help, Stephanie!" she said, laughing, and she tried to get around the couch to dodge Daddy, but he caught up to her and tickled her without mercy. "Stephanie, tickle him, tickle him!" Lynn yelped.

I hesitated a minute, then ran up behind Daddy and started tickling him under the arms.

"Whoa!" Daddy turned around so fast I almost got an elbow in the head. And then both Daddy and Lynn started tickling me at the same time. I screamed and wriggled, and we all lost our balance and fell on the sofa. I was breathless and laughing, and my legs and arms were all tangled up with Daddy's and Lynn's. For a minute I forgot about how mad I felt and let happiness flow everywhere in my body like a warm wave.

"We are going down the Nantahala, folks, and that's my final answer," Daddy said with a chuckle. "Nobody calls me a chicken."

"What about a pigeon? Has anybody ever called you a pigeon?" said Lynn.

I took a deep breath. The music on the CD went weaving all around us like a silk ribbon. I wanted Daddy to see the good parts of me, not just the parts that were scared.

The screen door squeaked and then slammed. Diana was standing in the doorway with an annoyed expression on her face.

"What are you guys doing?" Diana's voice sounded mad.

"Nothing," Daddy said. "Just a little family tickle-fest. Come on and join us."

"No way," said Diana. "You guys look ridiculous." She headed on up to the loft.

"Hey, we're going on a family white-water rafting trip day after tomorrow. Norm's going to sign us up," Lynn said to her. "Won't that be fun?"

"I'm not going," said Diana from the top of the stairs. "I'm riding every day."

"No, this is going to be a family thing, sweetie; we're all going," said Lynn.

"Not me," came Diana's voice from deep in the loft bedroom.

"Just a minute, young lady; you stop right there," said Lynn. She untangled her arm from around me and sat up, looking upstairs.

"What?" said Diana, looking down at us over the loft railing.

"When I want to talk to you, you don't just walk away. Come back downstairs," Lynn said, and this time she said it louder.

"No!"

Lynn stood up with her hands on her hips. "Diana, let's not get in a big argument about this. This is a family vacation and our whole family is going to go whitewater rafting. Including you. You'll get to ride plenty."

"First of all, we are not a 'family,'" Diana said, holding her hands and making air quotations. "Second of all, I'm not arguing. I'm just not going." She glared at all of us and turned away.

I didn't care whether Diana went rafting. I wanted out myself. But I couldn't imagine saying all that stuff that Diana was saying.

"Diana, your mother told you to come downstairs." Daddy's voice was louder than usual.

"You have nothing to do with me!" Diana said.

I glanced at Daddy's face and saw it turn all red. I curled into a tight ball in the corner of the couch.

"Diana!" Daddy was shouting now. "Come downstairs

right this minute and apologize to your mother for being disrespectful."

"I'm not doing anything!" Diana's mad face showed above the railing again.

Daddy got white spots on his cheeks and he pointed his finger at her. I could only remember one time he'd gotten this mad before, and that was at Mama. "And you WILL go rafting with the rest of this family day after tomorrow."

"I will not!"

"You will come down here now!"

"You can't tell me what to do!" Diana yelled.

"Norm, calm down, let me talk to her," Lynn said, touching Daddy's arm.

Daddy yanked his arm away from Lynn. "I won't put up with this kind of behavior!" he told her, then shouted upstairs. "That's it, you won't set foot in that barn for the rest of the week!"

"No! I hate you!" Diana screamed and ran back into the bedroom.

Lynn ran her fingers through her hair and whispered to Daddy. "Norm, calm down."

Daddy glared at Lynn. "You don't think she needs to be punished after talking to us like that?"

"No, of course she needs to be punished, but grounding her from the barn for the rest of our vacation is just extreme. That's all she lives for."

Daddy used his regular voice. "Well, give me a minute to calm down. I realize I lost my temper. We should always act with love, I realize that."

I tried to be silent and invisible as I slid off the couch and climbed the stairs.

"Listen, Norm, she's a difficult child. It's hard to deal with her."

"Fine, I won't. I'm going for a walk."

"We can't be fighting about these things in front of the kids."

"Fine. Come with me."

Lynn glanced up at the loft, and then followed Daddy to the door. The screen door slammed behind them, and their voices got fainter as they headed down the pine needle path. From the top of the stairs I watched the flashlight bob through the trees, shooting beams every which way as Daddy waved his hands around, complaining to Lynn. Daddy and Mama never fought like this. They just didn't talk, period. I didn't know which was worse.

I wanted to leave. Go outside and crawl into a hole somewhere. I knelt on my bed, watching Diana cry her eyes out.

"I hate him, I hate him, I hate him! All I want to do is ride! I wish Mom had never met him!"

I felt heat in the back of my skull, hearing Diana say that about Daddy, but I couldn't help thinking that I kind of hated him right now, too.

And just that very minute, I realized I'd also wished Mama had never met Barry, only I'd never dared to say it out loud. There was something really true about a lot of what Diana said. I felt like I should tell her.

"You know," I said to Diana. "I know what you mean. I used to feel so sure about Mama's love before she got married to Barry, and ever since then I sometimes wonder if now I come in second to him."

She blinked and looked at me for a second, then rolled away from me.

I sat on the edge of Diana's bed and watched her cry. I wanted to pat her on the back or touch her hair, but Diana was so mad I was almost afraid she might bite or scratch me. Finally I reached out my hand and stroked Diana's arm. It felt hot and damp.

"I don't think he should try to make you go," I said, and my voice sounded all scared and teeny, which made me madder at myself. "It's a vacation." I pulled my hand back but swallowed and went on. "I bet Daddy'll change his mind. Lynn'll talk him out of it."

Diana didn't answer.

I heaved a sigh. Downstairs, the music played, and a woman's sad voice sang about a girl on her own for the first time, making breakfast by herself. I wiped my wet face but tears just kept sliding out of the corners of my eyes.

11

DIANA

I slid out from under the thick comforter, yanked jeans and a sweatshirt over my pajamas. I glanced at Stephanie, asleep in the next bed. Carrying my shoes, I tiptoed down the stairs past Mom and Norm's closed door. In the kitchen, I grabbed the flashlight from the counter and went out onto the front porch.

Outside, the near-full moon shone like a silver coin in the dark sky. The mountain air felt unbelievably cold for July. I sat in one of the ancient rocking chairs to put my shoes on, but it squeaked. I lowered myself to the edge of the porch. I tied my shoes, then hurried, shivering in the clammy darkness, across the gravel parking lot toward the lodge.

I'd been so mad! So freaking mad! Almost like little sparks going off behind my eyes. Everything seemed sharp and bright and hard. And I felt a mean, hard dullness in the pit of my stomach.

A definite nine point seven five on the Moronic Mood-o-Meter. Dr. Shrink would be so proud that I stopped to figure that out, wouldn't she?

The bad part wasn't Norm yelling at me. It was that Mom hadn't even stood up for me. For all of my life, it had been me and Mom against the world. Now everything felt hopeless, like Mom was never going to be on my side again. So, I was going to do this one thing. Then I was running away to Dad's house in Florida. And never coming back.

As I headed toward the lodge, the wind in my face felt cold. A full moon slid from behind the clouds and lit up the high valley nestled in the pine-forested peaks. Moonlight hit the roofs of the barn and the cabins. It spilled like milk across the sloped grazing pastures, highlighting the white salt blocks that the cows and horses licked. I could swipe a bike from the front of the lodge and ride it almost the whole way to the wolves' pen. I'd only have to climb on foot over a rock formation the last twenty yards or so.

I grabbed the handlebars of one of the bikes, and gravel crunched under the tires as I backed it out of the rack.

"Diana! Wait!"

I turned around and saw Stephanie, hurrying to close the thirty yards between us.

"What the heck are you doing?" Anger raced through me like the wick on a stick of dynamite.

"You can't do this! You can't! Please!" Stephanie had on only her pajamas and a pair of flip-flops. What an idiot. She was going to freeze. She grabbed another one of the bikes.

"You don't even know what I'm doing!" I turned away. Pushed off. I couldn't believe this. Maybe, if I rode fast enough, I could lose her.

Icy wind stung my cheeks as I raced downhill toward the ranch entrance and took a hard right, ignoring Stephanie's shouts. But as I headed up the trail I'd found this afternoon, now lit with patches of bluish moonlight, I started having doubts. If Stephanie ended up lost and scared on the side of the mountain somewhere, guess who Mom and Norm would blame. Duh. I skidded to a stop. Straddled the bike. "What do you want?"

"Let me come with you." Stephanie peddled up the trail, then dropped one foot to the ground. Her whole body shivered in the thin pajamas.

"You have no idea what I'm doing."

"Yes, I do. You're runnin' away."

"What do you care? Once I leave, you could have Mom and Norm all to yourself."

Stephanie's mouth dropped open, like this was all totally news to her. "What are you talkin' about? Come on, let me come. I feel like I know how you feel about things."

"You don't even know me. We barely know each other at all."

"Hey, I really felt sorry for you after Daddy yelled at you tonight. I mean, I knew what you were talkin' about. I was on your side."

I had one foot up on the bicycle pedal. Now I put it back down. "So what. That doesn't change anything."

"If you run away, where would you stay? What are you gonna eat? How are you gonna get around?"

"I don't want to talk about it." I started pushing my bike up the hill. "Before I go, I have something else to do first."

"What?" Stephanie pushed her bike up behind me.

"None of your business."

"If you don't let me come, I'll tell 'em you sneaked out tonight."

"Yeah, but so did you!"

"But I'm followin' you, tryin' to get you to come home."

"Home. That's a laugh."

Suddenly a wolf howled. Another one joined in the singing, the two sad voices lacing their way through the treetops to the scattered stars.

I lifted my head and listened and caught a sudden glitter in Stephanie's eyes.

"You're gonna let the wolves go, aren't you?" Stephanie whispered.

I waited a minute too long before saying, "What are you talking about?"

Stephanie pushed her bike up beside me. "You think Russell's daddy mistreats them. I saw the way he yanked the chain."

I met Stephanie's gaze. Stephanie's entire body shook with the cold, but somehow she kept steady eye contact.

"Well, I'm not waiting for you."

"I'll keep up."

"And don't get in my way."

"I won't."

I started back up the hill. This might be a huge mistake. But what could I do? It was too late now. I couldn't take Stephanie back. I stood up on the bike pedals as the path got steeper. Stephanie's breath behind me was coming in high-pitched bursts. Man, she irritated me.

I thought back to the time I'd hung out with Russell back at the lodge. With animals, he was the way I'd always wanted to be. Like a magnet. The wolves trusted him, stood close to him, lay down at his feet. I hadn't wanted to leave.

At one point I'd crouched very low on the ground and moved very slowly and, at last, Oginali allowed me to touch her head with the tips of my fingers.

Would you like to go free, girl? Would you?

One of the adults had asked Russell if Oginali and Waya ever tried to escape.

"Every day," Russell had said.

The path got narrower. The straight trunks of pines closed in more tightly on either side. Not far away, an owl screeched. Something—probably a bat—flew too close to my head with an eerie, muted fluttering. I shivered.

And then, again, I heard the howls. Two voices, long and high and lonesome. I stopped. Glanced up at the moon, which was half hidden by a single gray cloud. Russell had said that wolves' howling at the moon was a myth and that they hardly howled at all. He'd said sometimes people heard coyotes and thought they were wolves. But that sure seemed like it came from the direction of the wolf pen.

"Diana?" Stephanie's voice behind me sounded scared. I ignored her.

The trail got so steep I had to walk the bike the last twenty yards to the foot of the rock face. Then I laid it on its side. I could see the gleam of the metal mesh fence just over the rock's summit. My ears and the tip of my nose were so cold they hurt. I cupped my fingers over my mouth. Blew on them.

"I'm so cold." Stephanie's whining was driving me batty. Her teeth were chattering and I wanted to knock them out. She dropped her bike on the path. I found hand and footholds, pulled myself up to a narrow ledge on the rock face. Stephanie was never going to get a foothold wearing flip-flops.

"Just stay at the bottom," I said. "If you try to climb you'll fall."

"No," said Stephanie. "I want to come."

I gritted my teeth. Let out a howl of frustration. Then, finally, I crouched on the ledge. "Put your right foot there, on that little place that sticks out." She actually did it. "Now put your hand on that bump and pull up. Good. Okay, now take my hand."

I reached down, clasped Stephanie's cold fingers, and pulled. I felt my weight start to pitch forward. For a second I thought I was going to fall. I scrambled backward, pulling Stephanie halfway up, then sat down hard. I grabbed Stephanie's wrists. "Can you get up now? Move your feet around and find somewhere to put your toes."

Stephanie flailed with her legs. She finally found a place for her foot, and scrambled, on her stomach, until she was lying halfway on the ledge. "I think my toes are bleeding," she said. She wedged one knee up over the edge, pulled herself into a sitting position. "Omigosh, I can't look down."

"Then don't." I started up the narrow rocky path, reached upward. If I said another thing to her I might shake her teeth out. Hooked my fingers through the icy metal diamonds of the chain link fence. "Hold on to the fence," I told Stephanie. "The electric part is only those wires on top."

The blue moonlight caught the fence's diamond-shaped pattern. A sound separated itself into a low growl.

"What's that?" Stephanie's voice held panic.

"The wolves, duh."

Stephanie made a frightened sound. "Keep climbing," I said. Using the bottom of the fence for hand-holds, we were able to climb sideways the rest of the way up the slope. The growling got louder.

I stood, finally on level ground, and scanned the darkness inside the pen. Would the wolves' eyes glow in the dark, like a cat's? Stephanie came up behind me, grabbed me by the elbow. She was shaking so much and standing so close that her knees were bumping my calves.

"Where are they? Can you see them?" The growling stopped.

I unpeeled Stephanie's fingers from my elbow. "Not yet. Let's walk around the edge and find the gate." We started around the pen. There was a tree inside, and a few rocks, but none close to the fence. Russell had said the wolves could climb anything close to the fence and get out.

Stephanie pointed to a shadowed structure back in the woods about forty yards away. "Is that Mr. Morgan's cabin?"

I looked through the woods at the darkened cabin. "Oh! Yeah, it must be."

"We don't want to wake him up."

"Thanks, Sherlock." No wonder she makes straight A's.

"So, are you just going to open the gate, or what?"

"I don't know. Russell said his dad had to put a couple of locks on there. I don't know if I can get it open. He said once these scientists did this experiment to see who was smarter, a wolf or a dog. They left each one in a closed garage and left a garage door opener on the floor. After four hours, the German shepherd was asleep in the garage, waiting for someone to come let him out. Guess how long it took the wolf to figure out how to work the garage door opener."

"I don't know. An hour?"

"Try ninety seconds."

"No, really? Did you make that up?"

"No, I swear, Russell said it was a real experiment. Wolves are smart."

"That is amazing," Stephanie said. She looked into the dark pen, more curious now.

I looked, too. Was something moving?

"What's gonna happen when they get out?" Stephanie asked.

"I don't know." I wished she would quit asking stupid questions. "No one will ever see them again."

"Won't Russell and Maggie miss them?"

I stopped and stared at Stephanie, opened my mouth to answer, then closed it and kept walking. "He wanted me to do this. He'd do it himself if he could, I know it."

"What if they attack us when they get out?"

"NO! They'll just run away."

"Are you sure?"

"No!" Halfway around the pen, we found the gate, which was secured with two combination locks and a length of thick chain. I yanked on them both. Neither gave. I glanced over at the cabin in the woods. Still dark.

The growling started up again. Two shadows melted out of the darkness. Oginali was flat on the ground and

Waya sat nearly motionless, watching us. They could have been statues.

Then Waya stepped forward. Moonlight painted the tips of her fur a milky blue. Her eyes gleamed a translucent greenish-orange. The moment spun out slowly as I met her narrowed eyes. I knelt, curling my fingers through the fence.

"Hey, Waya. Hey, girl. It's me, Diana," I said to the darkness. "Come on over." I stuck my hand through the enclosure.

"Diana! Are you crazy?"

"I don't think they'll bite me." I held my hand still, remembering Waya's nose touching it earlier tonight, and I held it out for Waya to sniff.

Waya took one step closer. Changed her mind and started to pace. Her ears, eyes, and nostrils seemed like a living computer, collecting information with lightning speed.

I started thinking out loud. "We could dig a hole under the fence. If we dug a small hole, maybe the wolves would even finish the job."

"Wouldn't we need a shovel?" Stephanie crossed her arms and clamped her hands under her armpits to warm them.

I glanced at the wolves. Waya was still pacing, kind of growling. Oginali slunk into the shadows.

"What about a log?" said Stephanie. "We could lean it up against the fence. They could walk up it."

I stared at Stephanie. Could she have actually come up with a decent idea?

"Not bad. C'mon, help me look for a log."

"Seriously?" Stephanie hesitantly followed me into the woods.

I scanned the dark ground with the narrow beam of the flashlight. I found one log, but it fell apart when I tried to move it.

"Diana, I'm so cold, I can't feel my hands or feet," Stephanie said. Whined is more like it.

"It was your idea to look for a log."

After another minute of searching I found a skinny tree leaning at an angle. It had fallen and been caught by the branches of another tree. It had a narrow trunk, only about four inches across. I worried it wouldn't be wide enough, but at least we could carry it.

I hoisted up the lower end. Propped it on my hip. "C'mon, lift the other end."

"It might have splinters," said Stephanie. "Or bugs."

I glared at her.

Stephanie sighed. She put her hands on the trunk and quickly removed them. "There's something slimy on there."

"Stephanie!" I hissed. Then I don't know why, I just started laughing.

102

Stephanie looked at me wide-eyed, then she started laughing, too. "Fine, I'm prissy, I admit it." With that she took both palms and slapped them firmly on the trunk. "Okay, go." She groaned and then staggered backward when she tried to lift the tree, but finally managed to get it balanced, and we worked our way out of the woods. We made a huge amount of noise, crashing through leaves, fighting branches, snapping sticks. I double-checked again to make sure the cabin was still dark. So far so good.

At last we got the trunk out onto the path. Panting and sweating now even in the cold, we lugged the tree back to the fence.

"We're going to slide this log over the fence into the pen," I said. "You have to help me, Stephanie."

She didn't say anything, and for a moment I worried she might turn around and run back to the cabin, but then she whispered, "Okay."

I was surprised by a sudden surge of emotion starting in my chest and trying to work its way up and out, but I swallowed it down and said, "Okay, on my count, lift and slide it over." I took a deep breath. "One, two, three, lift!"

We pushed the end of the log up, over the fence. I shoved. The end of the log slid past the fence top, its center passed over, and then the log tipped downward.

Our side rose up out of reach like a seesaw. Now the log was moving on its own. It hit the ground with a dull scraping sound and remained solid, leaning against the fence.

"Whew." I searched the pen for the wolves but all our noise must have scared them. They were nowhere in sight.

"Waya? Oginali? C'mere, girls, c'mon," I said, kneeling. Nothing. I glanced over at Mr. Morgan's cabin, still dark and silent. Found a rock about fifteen yards away from the fence and sat on it. My heart was pounding like a freight train, and I felt completely alive. I watched the moon-bright sky just above the spot where the log met the fence, the place I thought I might see the wolves' silhouettes right before they jumped to freedom.

Stephanie sat down next to me. "So, you think they'll jump?"

"If it was me, I would."

We waited, beginning to notice the noisy woods around us. Wind rustled leaves, an owl hooted not far away, crickets made a racket, and every minute or so a frog burped.

"The stars are so much brighter here than at home." Stephanie wrapped her arms around her knees to warm herself. "That was kind of cool what Maggie said today, about the Cherokees believing that the Milky Way was the Path of Souls."

"I wasn't listening," I said. I did notice now, though, that here on the mountain the stars did seem nearer to the earth. And though I knew that outer space was freezing cold, the stars winked in what seemed to be a warm, comforting way.

Stephanie leaned her head back and scanned the blanket of stars above us. She pointed at a dense band arching across the heavens like a luminous cloud. "That must be the Milky Way. I wonder which constellation has the Dog Star and which is Antares, the one they called the Great Mother Wolf."

"I don't know," I said, surprised that she'd remembered the names.

"Russell said that if the spirits don't like you, your soul can get stuck there, in the Milky Way."

"That's a boatload of stuck souls," I said. I wondered how many thousands of stars made up that swirling arch?

"Yeah," said Stephanie. "Sometimes I feel stuck, because I'm, you know, so scared of stuff. I wish I was as brave as you are."

I pretended the compliment didn't matter, but I felt my arms prickling with pleasure in the dark. "Well, you're brave with people," I said. "I wish I could be more like that."

"Well, Daddy always taught me to be kind, so I just try to do that, that's all." Stephanie said.

"You make it sound so easy." My throat tightened. Stephanie had no idea how hard it was.

"Well, ridin' is easy for you. So maybe being brave is doing stuff that's hard for you."

I couldn't believe it. The ache in my throat was like a burn. I was about to cry. I couldn't let Stephanie see. I turned away. Took deep breaths, thankful for the darkness and the cold.

"And what about what Maggie said about everyone having a reflection in a star?" Stephanie asked. "You know, what the Cherokees believe. I like the idea of having my own star up there. I think I'd pick the North Star," Stephanie added, "because that's the star people use to find their way home."

While Stephanie was talking, I wiped my cheeks and took a breath. "There it is, at the end of the Little Dipper." I pointed. "Mom showed me, in case I was ever lost."

"Yeah," Stephanie said. "Daddy taught me, too. If you know which way is north, then you can figure out all the other directions."

We sat for a minute without talking.

"That's kind of cool, that our parents both taught us where the North Star is, huh?" Stephanie said.

"Yeah, sure." I blinked. In a minute I might do something really stupid. Like cry more. The next second I heard something move, and the electric whooshing sound of a body hurling through the air. We turned and saw Waya arcing across the sky above us, the eerie cloud of the Milky Way behind her, moonlight brushing her eyes and teeth and fur. She landed silent as a ghost. She stared us down in a timeless way that seemed like hours, but was still only a fraction of a second. Then, like mountain mist, she melted into nothingness.

A streaking shadow followed just behind.

Something in the universe shifted. The stars slid out of focus, the sky seemed to lighten a bit.

I took a breath. I was shaking. The wolves were free. Soon, I would be, too.

12

STEPHANIE

I turned on the little nightlight by the bathroom sink and sat on the edge of the bathtub. Trying to be quiet, I ran a thin trickle of water to rinse the blood and dirt from my feet. I bit my lip when the water stung the cuts and scrapes.

My heart still pounded like crazy when I thought about riding on the bikes so fast in the darkness, about climbing that rock face, about lifting that gross log over the fence. About the glimpse I'd gotten of one of the wolves' sharp white teeth reflecting the moonlight.

I thought about Diana leaning down from the top of the rock face and saying, "Take my hand." And then later, when I came up with the idea to move the log, she seemed impressed.

That had been so cool, Diana and me just sitting on that rock, talking about the stars like good friends. I understood Diana better now. Diana was afraid her daddy didn't care about her, and now she was wondering about her mama. Being around Diana had forced me to admit that I was afraid of the same stuff myself. I was always trying to pretend those feelings weren't there, and she just came out and talked about them. I had a feeling she'd been about to talk to me about stuff that was going on with her, but then it seemed like we didn't really have to.

I was proud of myself for not giving up on Diana. I felt like we'd really become closer, and I felt like Daddy would be pleased.

I dampened a washcloth and wiped off my arms. I probably had bugs and cobwebs all over me. Yuck. I wished I could take a shower, but Daddy and Lynn might wake up. I let warm water run over my feet for another minute, then patted them dry, real gently, with a towel. They felt so raw. Putting on a pair of boots tomorrow would be torture.

Finally, I tiptoed into the bedroom and slid under

the covers. The other bed was empty. When we'd gotten back from freeing the wolves, Diana had said she was going on the early morning advanced trail ride with Maggie. She'd grabbed her riding boots and got ready to leave again. "Tell Norm and Mom where I've gone," she said. "And thanks for your help."

"You're welcome." I was pretty sure I'd convinced Diana not to run away, and that felt pretty good.

The glow on the side of Diana's face from the nightlight in the bathroom made her features look weird and a little bit scary. "You know you can't tell anyone about the wolves. I mean anyone. Not your dad. Not my mom. Especially not Maggie or Russell. No one."

"I won't," I said. Then I added, "Maybe you should comb your hair. Maggie might get suspicious if it's all full of sticks and leaves."

Diana had acted like that didn't matter and headed down the steps, then changed her mind. She'd come in the bathroom, combed her hair and washed her face, and then gone back downstairs again. I listened to the squeak of the screen door and the soft click of the lock as Diana left. Then it had been silent as snowfall.

13

DIANA

As soon as I got out of earshot, I pulled Mom's cell phone from my pocket. I'd noticed some people from the lodge standing under a certain tree on a hill to talk on cell phones. Figured that was a spot where I'd get service. The light was grayish, the way it is in the hour before the sun comes up. I hiked to the tree and stood up against the trunk so no one could see me. I called Dad.

"Hello?" Dad's voice sounded growly.

"Dad? It's me."

"Diana! What's the matter? Are you okay?"

"Yeah, I'm fine. I just … was thinking I'd come for a visit."

"Diana, do you have any idea what time it is?"

"Oh, sorry." My heart started squeezing itself. Dad sounded mad. "Well, you know, I've been texting you about coming to visit, but you didn't text back."

"Uh, Diana, things aren't great here right now." His voice sounded thick with sleep.

"What do you mean?"

"It's not a good time," he said, sounding very groggy.

"Why?" I asked. He didn't say anything. I waited for him to answer. "Dad?" Still nothing. "Dad!"

"Wh … Diana! It's five thirty in the morning!"

"I want to come stay with you," I cried. I felt the corners of my eyes prickling. The pounding in my ears grew louder. "Why didn't you answer my texts?"

"It's complicated," he said.

"I could take a train," I said. I felt desperate. "Kids travel by train on their own all the time, if you could just give me a credit card number."

"Are you out of your mind?" he asked. "Your problem is you don't think things through!"

He sounded so mean. I wished I was Waya, that I could tear something apart with my teeth. "I can take care of everything on my own," I said. "You won't have to worry about anything, if you could just give me a credit card number ..." My arms started shaking, and I hugged myself.

"Work is really stressful. A visit is out for now."

At that moment, I hated him. I wanted to smash the phone on a rock. I hated Dad's guts.

After a long silence, I heard Dad take a deep breath. "How's the riding?" he asked, more calmly.

I couldn't help myself. The words flew out of the intense rage lodging itself deep inside my chest. "I hate you!" I shouted.

"That's it, I'm hanging up. I've got enough problems. I don't have to listen to this. And don't call at five thirty in the morning like this. It makes me think something terrible has happened."

Something terrible *has* happened, I thought. I wanted to scream. I wanted to jump off the mountain. I slammed the cell phone to the ground. I punched the tree and screamed as loud as I could as a wave of fire traveled up my arm. Hot, angry tears burst from my eyes.

I stared off to the east where brightness began to spread across the horizon. I was wide awake, probably because I hadn't taken my meds, but I felt like every ounce of my energy was drained out, like I was a wet sack of sand. Moronic Mood-o-Meter crashed from the red zone down to about two point six.

At the sound of wheels on gravel I looked toward the lodge and saw Maggie park and get out of her black truck. I wiped the tears off my face. She spotted me and waved me over. There wasn't a whole lot I could do except head over there. I couldn't visit Dad. Where would I go? I had no idea what to do now. I'd need a day or so to figure that out.

"You doin' okay, Miss Diana?" Maggie asked. She smiled at me.

I knew she could tell I'd been crying, but she didn't say a thing.

"You're quite the early bird this mornin'. Come help me saddle up. A married couple was supposed to go on the advanced trail ride with us, but they canceled at the last minute. It's just you and me." I stood watching as Maggie headed down the path to the barn, assuming I was coming. "I bet you want to do some galloping, don't you? I can tell you've got a way with the horses."

Galloping! If I said no, she'd get suspicious, and the thought of galloping made something flicker in my chest. A spark. I found my feet falling into step beside Maggie, our boots scuffing the pebbly surface of the dirt road to the barn. When Maggie opened the barn door, a stripe of pale morning sun fell on the two barn kittens, one tabby and the other black with white feet and a white face. They stretched, blinking, and tumbled out of the stack of horse blankets where they were sleeping with their mother. They followed me around, scuffling with each other to get my attention.

I felt funny; I could feel everything starting to zoom around, up and down. It was like the blood was louder pulsing through my veins, like a waterfall in my ears. But being in the barn, going through the familiar horse routine, gradually calmed me down. I helped Maggie saddle up Copper and Chief Tenkiller and felt proud when Maggie complimented my confidence and knowledge.

Fifteen minutes later I was racing on horseback behind Maggie across the high mountain meadow. The wind whipped through my hair, and it seemed to blow away all the pain. My heart pounded with the rhythm of Copper's hooves. Not far ahead was Chief Tenkiller's tail, like a white flag. And just above it Maggie's long gray braid thumped her back like a Cherokee drummer. Maggie rode like she was part of the horse.

Now THIS was riding. Galloping, free of gravity, free of the earth, practically flying.

Maggie had seen me crying, but she hadn't asked a single question.

I imagined the wolves, right this minute, running free on the mountain, exploring woods and meadows, drinking from streams, climbing rocks to check out their territory. Maybe just inside that row of trees they were moving in and out of shadows, their gray coats nearly invisible, and their yellow eyes absorbing everything.

Up ahead, Maggie slowed the Chief to a walk. The meadow narrowed into a trail that wound down the mountain and through the woods again. Copper trotted right up behind the Chief and began to nose his way up past his flank. I saw the Chief turn his head sideways, threatening, and I wanted to gallop right by. My heart was kind of skipping.

It was like slowing down a team of oxen, but I reined Copper in. At the same time, Maggie made that strange sweeping gesture with her arm I'd seen the first day on the mountain. Copper stopped on a dime and walked along innocently just like he'd never tried anything.

"What is that motion you make?" I asked. "Copper gets right back in line."

"It's a version of horse whispering." Maggie turned in her saddle as Chief Tenkiller picked his way over rocks and tree roots on the path, in and out of shadows and sun. "I taught myself several years ago. Wish I could have used it yesterday with your sister, but I was just too far up the trail."

"I'd love to know how to do that. It would be like really talking to animals."

"It's all based on the idea of the herd, the pecking order. Usually the number one horse in the pack is the alpha mare. You know that from your time at the barn, right?"

"Right." As Copper walked, I let my backbone relax into his gait. The saddle squeaked rhythmically. Bugs and butterflies darted through the columns of sun slanting through the trees. "Is Chief Tenkiller high in the pecking order?"

At that moment Chief Tenkiller's silky tail arched. He let fly with a couple of clumps of grassy yellow dung without missing a step.

Maggie guffawed. "Oh, yeah, can't you tell what a classy guy he is?"

I laughed, too.

"He's big," Maggie continued. "But he's a teddy bear. The alpha mare in our barn is named Duchess. She's a skinny red mare who is quite the witch. But the thing with horse whispering is you telling the horse that *you're* the alpha. Copper's pretty new to the barn, and I've been working with him some because he's just a big ol' mess, always trying to cause trouble." Maggie was still turned backward, one hand resting on the back of the saddle, the other propped on the pommel.

"So Copper thinks you're the alpha mare?"

"That's right."

"So, you act like a horse?"

"Sort of, yeah."

"Could you teach me how to do it?"

"You'll only be here a couple more days, and that's not anywhere near long enough to really learn it. I mean, I've been working on it for years. But there are books and tapes you can get when you go home."

"That would be fantastic." I stroked Copper's damp, solid neck.

"I'll write down some stuff for you before you go home. You've got a good feel for the horses, that's for sure." The skin around Maggie's brown eyes crinkled when she smiled. "You're a natural."

Maggie's praise was like sunshine on my hair and face. Like pouring warm water on the places that were still hurting after the phone call with Dad. Hoof beats pounded the path behind us. Maggie quickly collected Chief Tenkiller's reins. I tightened my hold on Copper. From around a bend in the path galloped a large gray I hadn't seen before. Russell was riding bareback.

"Gran!" he shouted. "Stop!"

Copper and Chief Tenkiller pricked their ears and danced into each other as Russell slowed the gray to a trot before stopping a few yards away. He was breathing hard. Without stirrups, his long legs hung down past his horse's ribcage.

"The wolves got out!" he cried. "They're gone!"

Maggie sat forward in the saddle. "What?"

"Someone let them go," said Russell. I could tell from his expression when he looked at me that he didn't even remotely suspect me. I remembered the way we'd talked last night, sitting with the wolves. The way Russell had laughed when Waya touched my hand with her nose. "She likes you," he had said. "And she doesn't like just anybody." I remembered the things I'd told Russell about third grade, the things I'd never told anyone.

Maggie demanded, "How do you know that?"

"Someone dropped a log into the pen and propped it up on the fence. All Waya and Oginali had to do was walk up the log and jump. Dad is going to be so pissed when he finds out."

"Hey, I've threatened to let them go myself a dozen times, but I'd never really do it. Not that I care about what your father thinks. But someone could kill them if they're out running free."

"I know," said Russell.

Kill them?

Maggie turned Chief Tenkiller around on the path. "I'm sorry, Diana, I've got to get back. I've got to figure out what to do about this."

In my imagination, Waya and Oginali slunk through the woods alongside us, stealing in and out of sight. Silent, listening, their hooded heads low and wary.

"They're wild animals—won't they be okay?" I tried to keep my voice neutral.

"Waya and Oginali don't know how to kill in the wild," said Maggie.

"Next thing you know they'll be raiding chicken coops," added Russell, ducking a low-hanging tree limb. "They're not scared enough of people."

"What do you mean, not scared enough?" Goosebumps pricked their way up the back of my neck into my hairline.

"Full-blooded wolves from the wild are terrified of people. They won't come near farms or communities," Maggie explained. "Hybrid wolves are used to people. They'll venture closer. If they're hungry, they'll raid a chicken house or even chase down somebody's cat."

"They'd eat somebody's cat?" I felt my face start to burn. I thought about the barn kittens. And Waya's razor-edged teeth.

"Yeah, if they're hungry," said Russell.

"And then you can count on some hotheads taking a shot at them," said Maggie, nudging Chief Tenkiller into a brisk walk. "You just wouldn't believe how much some people hate wolves."

We started the horses down the mountain, with Russell in the lead and me in between him and Maggie. I liked Russell and Maggie so much. I hadn't meant to do anything to them. I thought they'd be happy for the wolves to be free.

"Whoever let those wolves go could have signed their death warrants," said Maggie.

I looked at the way Copper's reins crossed my palms and felt coldness seep to the ends of my fingers and toes.

14

STEPHANIE

There was a gray lightness in the room. It was just about morning. I thought I was too wound up to fall asleep, but somehow I must have, because when I opened my eyes the room was bright, and I heard steps on the loft stairs.

Lynn's head popped up over the stairwell, and then she came up and sat on the bed. Her short blonde hair was matted, and she looked real worried. "Stephanie, did Diana tell you where she was going?"

"Yeah, she had an early morning ride with Maggie."

"Oh." Lynn stroked my arm through the covers, staring at Diana's empty bed. "Okay, I remember Maggie mentioning something at dinner last night. But Diana's supposed to be grounded from the barn."

"Maybe she forgot." Under the covers, I crossed my toes. It was stupid and babyish, crossing my fingers or toes when telling a lie, but I still did it automatically.

Lynn rolled her eyes. "I seriously doubt it. That was a pretty big argument we had last night. It would be kind of tough to forget about it." Lynn stood up. "And did you two talk before bed? How did she seem?"

"She seemed okay." I met Lynn's eyes for a second, then dropped my gaze. "But if something was bothering her she wouldn't tell me."

Lynn sat down on the bed again. "I'm sorry about the way Diana acts, Stephanie. I know you've tried really hard with her, and I do appreciate it. She has to learn to focus and control her impulses, and it's harder for her than for others. She also is feeling insecure right now, since your dad and I have gotten married. And I know she's tried texting her dad, and he hasn't answered."

"Why hasn't he?" I really wanted to know. As much as Daddy put pressure on me, I couldn't imagine him not answering texts or calling.

"Mmm … Diana's dad is going through a tough time, I think."

"Oh." I nodded. "I can tell Diana doesn't like it when you and I talk."

Lynn covered my hand with hers. "I just think she's hurting so much. It's like if an animal is wounded and you try to help it, it will try to bite you. Do you know what I mean?"

"I guess," I said, with a small smile. "My feelings aren't hurt."

"Well." Lynn rubbed my arm through the covers. "You are a very perceptive girl, Stephanie. Things okay with you, honey?"

So now she was trying to see how I was without letting me know that Dad had told her.

"I just want you to know, sweetie, that any time you want to talk, feel free," Lynn was saying. "I'd never try to take your mom's place, but if you do need or want someone to talk to, I'll be happy to listen. Why don't you get dressed and come on downstairs? You and your dad and I will go over to the lodge for breakfast. I bet Diana didn't even eat anything or take her meds before she left."

Had Diana taken her pill? I couldn't remember. I didn't think she had, but I didn't want to get her in trouble, so I stayed quiet.

"Is she really going to be grounded for the rest of the week?" I asked. "It doesn't seem fair."

Lynn cocked her head and looked at me thoughtfully. "You're pretty protective of your stepsister, even though she's not so nice to you."

I smiled and shrugged. Lynn patted my legs through the covers and then moved toward the door. "Well, your dad and I will discuss it. I'm going to go down and take a shower. Why don't you come on downstairs when you're ready?"

"Okay. I need to take a shower, too. I'll be down in a few minutes." I pulled the covers to my chin. I'd told enough lies just now to use up every one of my fingers and toes. If I said anything else I'd have to grow a couple of tails or something.

I put on socks and tennis shoes after my shower to cover up the scrapes on my feet. But when I got downstairs, the first thing Daddy said, looking up from the paper, was, "Morning, sweet pea. How'd you get those scratches on your arms?"

I looked down. "Oh, that must've been when Nick and I were playing horseshoes. I accidentally threw one of them in some bushes."

Daddy nodded. "Oh, well, you might want to put some Neosporin on those."

"Yeah, I will."

"Sometimes scratches like that can get infected."

"Right."

"Hungry, sweet pea?" Daddy put down the paper and pulled me to him in a big hug, hooking his arm around my waist. Daddy felt warm and smelled like aftershave.

"Uh-huh." I tried pulling away.

"Hey, kid, Lynn says I'm being too tough on you about riding. I wanted you and Diana to get closer, and I also want you to get better at riding, but my lovely wife says I'm putting on too much pressure. So, forget about riding today. We're on vacation. Relax."

"Thanks, Dad." Even though this was just what I wanted, now, somehow, I wasn't that excited.

"And about the argument last night," Daddy went on. "I shouldn't have lost my temper with Diana like that. I hope you understand. We can't allow her to talk back like that, but I admit I was out of line with my temper."

"Is she still grounded for the whole week?"

"Uh ... Lynn and I decided that if she goes rafting tomorrow, she only has to give up one day of riding. We think that's fair. Anyway, is she still asleep? Doesn't she want to eat breakfast?"

I glanced into the bedroom where Lynn was. Hadn't she said anything to Dad? "Uh, I don't know."

"Why don't you go upstairs and wake her up? Tell her the family is going over to the lodge to eat." Daddy glanced upstairs and then folded the paper. "Wait, I'm the one who lost my temper. Never mind, I'll go up and talk to her." Daddy stood up.

Suddenly it hurt me to breathe. What would happen when Daddy got upstairs and saw that Diana wasn't there?

Lynn hurried out of the bedroom, raking a brush through her hair. "That's okay, Norm, you don't need to do that. She's exhausted. Last night was kind of rough. Let's just let her sleep, why don't we?" She gave me a quick look. "I'll bring her back a plate from breakfast, and then I'll talk with her about rafting and being grounded from the barn for a day."

I swallowed, trying not to stare at Lynn. Lynn was lying to Dad! But she was trying to help Diana. Now there were two of us trying to help Diana and to protect her from Dad.

"Well, if that's what you want to do," Daddy said. "I just want to get everything back on the right foot." Daddy sat back down and picked up the paper again.

"We will," said Lynn. "But just let her sleep for now."

I went out on the porch without a word. I sat in one of the ancient rocking chairs, waiting for Daddy and Lynn to come outside. I didn't like that Lynn was keeping secrets from Daddy. Married people should tell each other the truth. But Diana and I weren't telling Daddy and Lynn the truth. I grabbed a hunk of my hair and twirled it tightly around my finger. I squeezed harder, making my finger throb.

From the porch, I could see the colorful patchwork patterns of the surrounding mountains. The mountains that were closest were green, the ones in the middle distance were dark purple, and the ones farther away were a lighter shade of purple. Somewhere loose in those mountains were two gray wolves with yellow eyes. I shivered, remembering the way that one wolf paced back and forth, back and forth, back and forth.

* * *

Nick and his parents joined us at breakfast as I was finishing my cereal. The wranglers handed around platters of fluffy scrambled eggs, sausages, and mountains of grits topped with pools of melted butter. Daddy was serving himself big helpings of each. Mama would have yelled at him to go ahead and eat like that, she'd just collect the insurance money once he keeled over from his clogged arteries, but Lynn didn't say a word. Daddy was telling Nick's parents about tomorrow's rafting trip, trying to talk them into going along.

I watched all of these ordinary events go on as if I

were inside some sort of bubble. Everything seemed so weird and surreal. I placed my hand on my cheek and felt my jaws moving up and down through the skin. I had aches and pains in odd places and my eyelids pricked from being up too late last night. The wolves were free. Diana and I had sat on a cold mountain rock talking about the stars. The whole world had changed. But no one else knew. On the surface everything seemed exactly the same.

Nick poked me under the table.

"Look," he said. In his hand was a yellowish-brown toad no bigger than a thumbtack. "Isn't he cool?" Sitting on Nick's palm, the toad looked tiny and lost on a huge pink field with deep crevices in it.

"You should let him go."

"I will," said Nick. "I just wanted to show him to you."

"What are you kids doing?" asked Nick's mom.

We looked up.

"Nothing," said Nick.

"Did you bring some sort of critter to the table?"

"Just a toad."

"A toad? Nick! Take that toad outside this minute, and then go wash your hands."

Nick made a face, then slowly got up. The wooden legs on his chair scraped as he pushed it under the table.

"Daddy, can I go with him to let it go?" I asked. "I'm done with my cereal."

Daddy and Lynn glanced at each other. "Sure," Daddy said.

I jumped up and followed Nick out the back door to the edge of the patio. Nick knelt. The toad hopped an inch across Nick's palm, then made a daring leap off and fell about a foot and a half to the ground.

"Whoa! That was probably like falling off a huge cliff to us," I said.

"Yeah. He looks kind of dazed." Nick laughed.

I thought about the cliff last night. What would Nick think about the wolves? He didn't have a big mouth. He wouldn't tell anyone. But would he think we'd done something wrong? I was absolutely crazy to tell.

"Guess what?" I said.

Nick didn't take his eyes from the toad. "What?"

The porch door slammed behind us. The toad scrambled under some plants and disappeared.

"What?" Nick said. "What were you going to tell me?"

Glancing through the window, I saw Mr. Morgan at the entrance of the dining room, talking in a real loud voice to the lodge manager. He yelled loud enough I could hear him all the way outside. His eyes were bloodshot, his gray-black hair was sticking up, and his shirt was buttoned up wrong. Coldness ran down my arms.

"Wait a minute." I touched Nick's arm. "I'll tell you later."

I stepped inside so I could hear Mr. Morgan. Nick was right behind me.

"Somebody let my wolf dogs go." Morgan was practically shouting. "Those wolves cost me three hundred dollars each. I know it was somebody from here. Somebody that heard the talk last night."

"Mr. Morgan, calm down. Come to my office, let's talk there." The lodge manager led Mr. Morgan out of the dining room.

"Whoa!" Nick said. "Somebody let the wolves go?"

I sneaked behind Nick into the narrow hallway where the restrooms were.

"Where are you going?" Nick asked.

I pointed at the restroom and ran inside. I looked at myself in the small mirror above the sink. My own brown almond-shaped eyes looked back, my smooth bronze cheeks, my mouth maybe a little more serious than usual. How could I still look the same as I'd looked yesterday?

So much had changed. I turned on the water full blast and started washing my hands.

15

DIANA

I dragged my feet up the stairs to the lodge porch. My eyes burned. Every muscle ached. I'd missed a whole night's sleep. On the ride back to the barn with Maggie and Russell, I'd realized that if I ran away it would be obvious that I'd been the one who let the wolves go. Like an advertisement, practically. So when they got back to the barn, I'd offered to take care of the horses. Put the tack away while Maggie and Russell went out in the pickup to search for Waya and Oginali.

"You're a peach, Diana," Maggie had said as she started the truck.

"Yeah, thanks, Diana," Russell said as he climbed in and slammed the passenger door. I'd smiled in a way Maggie and Russell probably thought was just modest. I watched the truck climb the hill to the back entrance of the lodge. Saw Russell's lanky figure jump out and sprint across the back patio.

The horses were damp and lathered from the ride back. I took my time brushing them and cleaning the tack. Copper nuzzled me for sugar and I gave him some. I stroked his soft, velvety muzzle and the smooth auburn disc of his jaw. I combed his mane and forelock in dreamy slow motion, as though I were styling my own hair. Every now and then he butted me, just for play, and I felt an ache in the back of my throat thinking about how attached I'd become to this horse in just a few days. His big brown eyes, when he looked at me, were liquid and peaceful.

Maggie had said to turn all three horses out into the pasture, so I did. I stood on the bottom rung of the fence and watched them trot away. Like kindergartners, they picked at each other but stayed together as they meandered through the yellow flowers. After a couple of minutes they all lowered their heads to graze. The other two horses stayed together. Copper grazed a little ways away. He tried moving closer. The other two edged away. Probably because he was one of the lowest on the pecking order. I hoped he would move up. I could feel the way he was trying.

I went back to the cabin. Found nobody there. Two days without my meds. I could feel the black cloud coming back over me, like those veils that some ladies wear to church in Italy. The zooming wasn't fun anymore. I felt sick to my stomach. I took a pill with some water.

My stomach growled. Maybe everyone was over at the lodge having breakfast. I realized I'd been up all night and then on a long morning ride without anything to eat. So I headed over. I should talk to Stephanie before I saw Mom and Norm, to see if anyone had missed me.

I went around to the hummingbird feeder, stood on my tiptoes. Peeked in the window. I saw Stephanie coming out of the women's room and signaled for her to come out onto the porch. Then I ran around to meet her.

Stephanie burst through the screen door with Nick right behind her and touched my arm, saying, "We didn't tell Daddy you went to the barn. He thinks you just got up."

"Really? Does Mom know?"

"Yes—but get this—she told Daddy you were still asleep."

Something fluttered in my chest.

"And guess what? Mr. Morgan came by a few minutes ago. He is really, really mad—somebody let his wolves go."

I glanced at Nick, then let my eyes grow wide with shock. "Really?"

"Yeah. He said they cost him three hundred dollars apiece."

I swallowed. I let my eyes slip over to Nick, then back to Stephanie, and Stephanie shook her head, just barely. She hadn't told him. "Gosh, I wonder who did it?"

"He thinks it was somebody who was at the talk last night," Nick offered.

"Wow. Is breakfast over? I'm starved."

"I think there's still some cereal and biscuits on the buffet table," said Nick.

"Hey, Nick, nobody would think it was weird for you to go get seconds, right?" Stephanie said.

"Not hardly," he said, grinning.

"Could you please, please get Diana a biscuit? So she doesn't have to talk to the 'rents?"

Nick gave Stephanie a funny look. Probably surprised to see us getting along.

But he said, "Well, okay," and went back inside.

"Oh, no," Stephanie said, the second he left. "What are we going to do? We're going to be in so much trouble. That man was so mad. And he seems like he's so mean, Diana."

"Maggie and Russell are mad, too! They went out looking for the wolves. And they think some of the farmers around are going to kill Waya and Oginali. This is terrible. Don't tell anybody yet, even Nick. We need time to figure this out. Okay? Swear?"

Stephanie looked like she might be sick, but she nodded. "Your mom wondered if you'd taken your pill," she said.

"I did." I didn't look at Stephanie. Looked out at the purple-hued angles of the mountains, pink-framed in the morning sky. I scanned the tree line, wondering if Waya and Oginali had stayed together. Or separated. I wondered how far a wolf could go in one day.

The screen door slammed.

"Here." Nick handed me a glass of orange juice and three warm, butter-soaked biscuits wrapped in a napkin.

"Oh, man, thanks; you're the best," I said. Saliva flooded my mouth and I ate half a biscuit in one bite and gulped the orange juice.

I was still eating when an old pickup truck pulled up a minute later. A tall man wearing a flannel shirt and faded jeans got out. He wore granny glasses, and his hair was longish and blonde with some gray mixed in. A silver refrigerator compartment occupied a third of the flatbed of his truck. Stacks of plastic containers and coiled lengths of ivory-colored rubber tubing filled the rest. Hanging out of one box was the longest rubber glove I'd ever seen. It looked long enough to go up to a person's shoulder.

His boots scuffed the front steps and he smiled at us. "Afternoon, folks," he said. "Maggie around?"

"She's out looking for some wolves," I said.

"I know; I'm Doc. She called me about it." Doc leaned against the porch railing. "I sure hope we can find those pups. I love those wolves. First time I went to vaccinate them I went inside their pen and was kneeling down to get the syringe, and Waya stole my dern medical bag. She ran around with it for a while, and I swear she was smiling. Then she dropped it and walked away, so I headed over to get it, and just as I'm leaning over to pick it up Oginali comes running by and grabs it. I ended up playing keep away with those two for half an hour. Course, there was nothing left of my bag."

"Hey, I didn't know wolves were playful," Nick said.

"Heck, yeah. I frankly don't know why people are so terrified of wolves. They're not so much vicious as they are mischievous. Course, these two, they'll never make it on their own."

"What do you mean?" Stephanie asked.

I was careful not to look at Stephanie while Doc explained the difference between hybrid wolves and real wild wolves. I'd never forget the way my heart was beating. In school we'd read this story by Edgar Allan Poe called *The Tell-Tale Heart* about how this guilty guy's heart was beating so loudly that he was sure everyone could hear it. My heart was beating like that now. But every minute that went by made it seem less and less possible to tell the truth.

"The bottom line is, these wolf-dogs shouldn't even exist," Doc said. "They're not very good as pets, and they can't survive in the wild. It's like there's no good place for them. Waya and Oginali should be living in one of the wolf rescue reserves near here. Maggie and I tried to explain that to Joe back when he got them, but he wouldn't pay attention. He thought he could make money on them. And now look at the mess we've got."

Maggie's truck spun around the corner and came to a sudden halt beside Doc's. Both doors flew open, and Maggie and Russell jumped out.

"Doc! Thanks for coming."

"Did you bring your gun?" Russell said.

"Yep." Doc took the steps two at a time and crossed to the bed of his truck. He reached in and took out a long black gun case.

I jumped to my feet. "You're not going to shoot them!"

"It's a tranquilizer gun," Doc said. He unzipped the case. Everyone crowded around. He pulled out a plastic container containing several darts with feathery yellow tails. "There's anesthesia in the darts. Puts them to sleep so we can get them back."

"I just hope you shoot them before anybody else does," said Maggie.

"That would be the idea," Doc said.

"We've tracked them heading in the direction of Scooter McGuff's farm, but then they must've waded down the creek a ways. We lost the track." Russell took the box of anesthesia darts Doc handed him and scanned the overcast sky. "Plus, it looks like it might rain, which would wash away the track."

"You two coming?" said Doc as he climbed in behind the wheel.

"Yeah," Russell said. "Hey, you ought to come," he said to me. "You're the one who has that telepathic thing going with Waya." He caught my eye. My heart kind of thudded. He raised his fingers in a good-bye gesture as Maggie swung into the cab. Doc backed the truck out onto the road.

Stephanie, Nick, and I watched in silence as a swirl of dust followed the truck down the dirt road. I glanced at Stephanie, whose eyes were wide and watery. With Nick here there was nothing we could say.

Just then Mom and Norm came out on the porch with their coffee cups. Mom came over and kissed my forehead, saying, "Oh, you're up, sweetie, did you catch up on your sleep?" I could tell Norm felt bad about yelling at me last night because he kept cutting his eyes at me with a half smile, but I also knew he wouldn't say anything with Nick around. Maybe Nick would hang around with us all day. Everyone would be polite. Pleasant. I wouldn't get interrogated.

"Hey, kids, how about a trip to Tweetsie Railroad?" Norm said in a jovial voice.

Tweetsie Railroad was for little kids, but considering how mad Mr. Morgan was, maybe going to Tweetsie Railroad was the perfect thing to do.

"Okay," I shrugged. "It's okay with me." I almost smiled when I saw the look of shock on Mom's face.

Stephanie looked a little surprised, too, but went along in a heartbeat. "Hey, that might be fun."

"Nick, would you like to come to Tweetsie Railroad with us?" said Mom.

"I'll ask," he said with a quick grin and headed inside the lodge, leaving the screen door swinging.

So, that's how we ended up driving down the mountain with Stephanie squeezed between Nick and me in the backseat. I noticed that when Nick had a choice of getting in the car beside me or Stephanie he picked Stephanie.

Stephanie and Nick played stupid games like saying "jinx" when they said the same thing or poking each other in the arm or saying "punch-buggy, no take-backs" when they saw a Volkswagen. Nobody poked my arm or said "jinx" to me so I just acted like it was stupid.

At Tweetsie Railroad we rode around in the woods in an old-timey train. Some guy with a mountain twang made lame announcements about how the Tweetsie Railroad was pretty dangerous. He hoped we came out of it alive. Once the train stopped, high school and college kids dressed in cowboy and Indian costumes faked a fight. Another time some so-called bandits with kerchiefs tied over their noses and mouths got on the train and walked up and down the aisle telling people to empty their pockets. Nick and Stephanie giggled as they swaggered by.

Norm embarrassed everyone by acting like he was in the scene, too. He stood up and said, "Citizens' arrest! Citzens' arrest!" He got one of the bandit college kids in an armlock, and when the kid with the badge jumped on board, he yelled, "I got this one for you, Sheriff!"

The sheriff was a little surprised. Looked at the bandits and laughed, but he went along with it. "Hey, good work, Pop," he said.

"Omigosh, I have never been so embarrassed in my life," Stephanie said. She ducked her head and hid her face on Nick's shoulder.

"Norm, you're embarrassing the kids; would you sit down?" Mom kept saying. But she was laughing in between her words. Everyone spent a lot of time trying to get me to laugh with them but I wouldn't. I couldn't. Even if some of the stuff was kind of funny. After the train there were a few other rides. Then we got hot dogs and funnel cakes and sat at a picnic table to eat them.

On the way home we stopped at a place beside the road where people could pan for gemstones. Norm bought everyone a big bucket full of dirt, each of which was guaranteed to have at least five gems, including emeralds and sapphires. I couldn't imagine my dad ever doing that. He would have called it a rip-off joint. Wouldn't even have stopped the car.

I watched Mom with Norm, the way they touched each other all the time, just lightly, like they owned each other. Mom and Dad had fought all the time. I never saw them touch. And Stephanie was smacking Nick's arm, hiding her eyes on his shirt. Nick was into it.

Well, so what. Boys in general could eat dirt.

We sat on wooden benches and poured the dirt, one handful at a time, into a trestle with water running over a screen. The water washed the dirt through the screen, and a few of the ordinary-looking rocks transformed under the stream of water to become vivid purple, amber, and tiger-striped gems.

And I couldn't believe it, Norm and Mom bought a bucket, too. They sat together with their shoulders touching. Sifting through the sand.

"It's like a rock makeover," said Stephanie, giggling. She held up a brown dirt-coated rock. "Before." She held up a shiny wet chunk of tigereye. "After."

Then Norm jumped up holding a brownish-looking rock and said, "Lynn, love of my life, we're rich. Now I can buy you that big screen TV you've always wanted!"

I watched Mom laugh. She sounded like a teenager. I didn't think I'd ever seen her laugh like that before. "Norm, that's a rock. A plain old rock. Would you please sit down?"

But Norm kissed the rock. Then kissed Mom. "And I know how much you've wanted that digital cable with eleven different sports channels, and now we can get that for you, too, honey." Norm hugged Mom. She couldn't stop laughing.

I heard Nick whisper to Stephanie, "That is just a rock, right?"

"Right."

"So, is your stepmom a big sports fan?"

And Stephanie laughed and said, "No, Daddy is. He's just acting stupid again."

Stephanie and I looked at each other. Tried to keep straight faces. The clouds had blown away and it had not rained at all. The afternoon sun blanketed my head and shoulders like warm hands. I got a little sleepy then, sitting on the bench, searching for hidden gems. Maybe it was my pill. But maybe it was just being there. Time spun by in a golden lazy way and I had to admit it was nice.

Moronic Mood-o-Meter steady on five point five.

Later in the afternoon Nick and Stephanie went to look at some arrowheads in a gift shop. I got a little nervous about Nick and Stephanie being together. Would Stephanie accidentally give something away? I was about to follow them when Norm came over. Put his arm around my shoulders.

"Sorry I lost my temper," Norm told me. "And your mom says grounding you from the barn for the whole week was too harsh. You had to skip riding today, and your mom says that's enough. We'll all go raftin' as a family tomorrow, and then you can ride the rest of the week. How's that?"

"That sounds okay," I mumbled. I stared at the

ground. Norm's arm hugged my shoulders, heavy and warm.

Later that night, I followed Stephanie into the loft bathroom and shut the door behind us. I turned on the fan so its noise would cover our conversation.

"You swear you didn't tell Nick?"

Stephanie looked up from brushing her teeth. She shook her head. Spit out toothpaste. "No!" she said. "I promised you, didn't I?" It was nearly ten. Stephanie had just taken a shower. Her long wet hair had made a dark half-moon on the back of her pajama top. "I didn't, I swear. But I feel so terrible." Stephanie put the top on the toothpaste. "I mean, I felt sorry for the wolves in that pen. I thought we were helping them. But it turns out we weren't."

I sat down on the closed toilet lid. "Let's face it, we weren't thinking about what we were doing." I heaved a sigh. Knew my face didn't look as confident as I wanted it to.

Stephanie sat on the edge of the tub. She rubbed her eyes, then wrapped a towel around her wet hair. "I don't know, maybe if we said we didn't know it was wrong. I mean, most people would think what we thought—that wolves are wild animals and shouldn't be in a pen. But look at all that Maggie and Russell went through today. Riding through the woods looking for them with Doc. And Maggie calling all the farmers and stuff nearby, telling them. And did you hear her at dinner telling what that one farmer said?"

"Yeah." I stared at the floor. "If the wolves come on his property they'll never leave alive. And someone at dinner said that Mr. Morgan's been driving around looking for them, too. I don't want him to get the wolves back! What if Mr. Morgan finds them before Maggie and Russell do?" I looked back up at Stephanie. "I wish we could go look for them ourselves."

"But how can we? We'll be gone rafting all day."

16

STEPHANIE

"You can call me Wild Wes. They let me out of the joint for good behavior on Monday, and I've been a river guide since Tuesday." The skinny, tanned guy at the front of the bus wore ancient jams and light brown dreadlocks. He had a real crazy smile. "This guide here is Jesse, who deserves a big round of applause for finally passing his lifesaving course after taking it seven times. Last but not least is Zeke. Yesterday was his first day back after an extended hospitalization, which occurred the last time he went down this river. Even though he's blind and deaf now, he will be able to guide you around the rapids using his acute sense of smell."

I pulled the straps tighter on my orange life vest. I poked Diana, next to me. "He's making that up, right?"

Diana nodded and laughed. "He's kidding, Steph."

Once Diana had figured out that rafting was kind of dangerous, she suddenly acted real excited about it. I was trying to look on the bright side.

The bus lurched as it pulled into a gravel parking lot just below the dam, and Wild Wes grabbed an overhead railing, showing off his tattoo of this coiled-up river monster on his upper arm. The bus pulled over to a place by itself on the corner of the lot. "This here dam is right on the Tennessee line. We have to park at this end of the lot because me and Jesse, we would be violating our probation if we left the state of North Carolina. But don't worry, you're going to be perfectly safe with us."

Everybody laughed, real nervously, as we stood up and filed off the bus. We looked like a bunch of big old bugs, standing around in our orange vests and helmets. Wild Wes assigned each group to a guide, then said to Daddy, "Your group goes with me."

"I guess we should say our last good-byes, then," Daddy joked.

"That's right," said Wild Wes with a big old grin. "If there's anything you've been meaning to say to your loved ones, best say it now. Don't hold back."

Daddy took Lynn by the shoulders and looked real deeply into her eyes. "Honey, I don't care for your meat loaf."

Lynn rolled her eyes at Diana and me. "I'm afraid it's going to be like this all day, girls." She put her hands on Dad's cheeks. "Sweetheart, put a sock in it."

I glanced at Diana to see how she was reacting. She rolled her eyes again but didn't seem too upset. I grabbed a handhold on the heavy, yellow, five-man raft and helped tote it down to the river's edge. Wild Wes led the way.

Sunlight went dancing across choppy waves in the river, and the water rushing by was as muddy as could be.

"It's not *too* cold," Diana said, standing up and flicking water from her fingertips.

I nodded and swallowed. I couldn't say a thing. I thought I would be all right until I'd gotten down here and actually seen the water.

"A little rafting lesson," Wild Wes said. His voice and face turned real serious. "All kidding aside, I've been going down the Big Pigeon twice a day about a hundred days a year for the past six years, which means I've been down this river more 'n a thousand times. I know every twist 'n turn, and I've ridden this river in every possible condition. The river's runnin' low this summer, which means you've got to be extra careful about rocks in the rapids. During this trip we'll hit two class four rapids. It's extremely important to pay attention and do what I say when I say it, no questions asked. You can't say, 'Why,' or 'In a minute.'" Wild Wes raised his eyebrows and looked at all of us. "Got it?"

We all nodded.

"If you follow my instructions you'll make it fine."

I tried to swallow again but my throat was so dry the spit got stuck. I reminded myself that after all Daddy's kidding around, he and Lynn had ended up picking the warm, safe Big Pigeon River over the cold and dangerous Nantahala.

Wild Wes explained that he would be sitting in the rear of the raft. Daddy and Lynn would sit toward the back, and Diana and I would sit up front. Wes showed us how to sit on the inflated cross-seats and wedge our feet under the curved inside wall of the raft. He explained that his command "Paddle forward" meant everyone should take long, steady strokes with our oars. "Paddle back" meant everyone should paddle backward, pushing our oars deep into the water. "Right back" meant those on the right side of the raft should paddle backward while those on the left paddled forward. "Left back" meant those on the left paddled backward, and those on the right paddled forward.

"If somebody falls out of the raft," Wes said, "do not jump in after them. Reach out to them with a paddle, or I'll throw them a rope. And if you fall out, the number one rule, the most important thing," he said with conviction, "is *never* stand up in the river. That's how people drown when they're white watering—they fall out of the raft and try to stand up and get their feet caught in the rocks. If you wipe out, float on your back facing down river with your feet up. *Do not stand up in the river!* Got that? Questions?"

"Have you ever wiped out?" Daddy asked.

"At least twice a week." Wild Wes grinned and made a terrified face.

"How reassuring," Daddy said. He squeezed my shoulder.

"All aboard!"

My knees shook a little as I climbed into the raft, and I nearly stumbled, but I kept on going. There was water in the bottom of the raft and my tennis shoes got soaking wet. It squeaked when I sat down. I wanted to lean back against Daddy so I could feel the solid warmth of his life vest behind me, but I was still mad at him, so I just sat very straight. Diana and Lynn, on the other side of the raft, looked happy in a sort of breathless way. Lynn reached forward and brushed Diana's hair from her face. Diana was scanning the shoreline around us. She didn't seem like she was listening to Wild Wes's instructions.

"Try not to drop your oar," Wild Wes said as he settled himself on the back end of the raft. "Because then we have to go back and get it, which is a pain in the you-know-what. But if you do, it floats. Don't panic. Here's how you hold it." He showed how to clasp the T-handle of the oar with one hand and place the other midway down for most efficient rowing. "See this above my eye?" He pointed at a white ,shiny scar on his forehead. "Projectile oar injury, the most common in rafting. Keeping your hand over the T-handle will save your fellow rafters from such a fate. When you're not rowing, lay the oar across your lap like this." He demonstrated.

I wedged my foot under the curve of the raft edge and placed the oar across my lap the way Wild Wes said. I took a deep, shaky breath and watched a dead branch bob by, yanked to and fro by the current. I said a little prayer to myself. *Dear God, please help me to be brave.*

"Okay, everybody ready?"

"Ready!" said Lynn and Diana.

Daddy and I didn't say anything.

Wild Wes laughed. "Hey, am I sensing more enthusiasm on one side of the raft than the other?"

"That is purely your imagination," Daddy said. "I'm pumped, aren't you, Steph?"

I glanced around.

"Come on, Stephanie," Lynn said. "This is going to be so much fun." She reached over and squeezed my knee.

"Yeah, it'll be fun," Diana said, giving me a nod.

That in itself made me feel better. "I'm ready."

"All right!" shouted Wild Wes. With a loud yodel, he shoved off from the riverbank, and our raft surged into the current. "All paddle!"

My heart beat double-time as I lowered my oar into the water and smacked right into Daddy's.

"Whoa! Wait, let's get our timing right," Daddy said. "Stroke, stroke, stroke."

The raft jerked as a group of high school boys in Jesse's raft careened into us on purpose, laughing and spraying us with water. I screamed my lungs out. My T-shirt got soaked.

"Hey, watch it, wise guys!" Wild Wes shoved the other raft away with his oar. "Paddle forward, get them out in the middle; let's lose these juvies," he shouted.

I paddled, and then Daddy started chanting "Stroke, stroke, stroke," which started to get on my nerves in about ten seconds.

"Good job. Stop."

I put my oar on my lap. The high school boys were ahead of us, trying to spray someone else. The raft went faster now that we were in the middle of the river. Rocks and trees slid by on the shore. Weeping willows and other river trees draped branches and tangled roots over the edge. Then we left them behind. The sunlight bouncing off the water and the rushing sound of the current made my brain buzz. Some of my fear leaked away.

"Hey, Steph, you're doing great!" Lynn said.

"Yeah, nice work, Steph," Daddy said. "You're doing a good job."

I glanced back and smiled at Diana, who was giving me the thumbs-up sign. I didn't know whether it was God who had given me the courage or not, but I had been brave.

17

DIANA

"Paddle forward!" Wild Wes shouted. "Class four rapids coming up! This is called Thunder Road! Stay right of the rock!"

The white water roared louder, and a rock the size of a bear was ahead of us, black and wet, right in the middle of the river. Just beyond bear rock churned the white froth of the rapids. I leaned into my oar and paddled with all my might. The raft skimmed across the water, heading right for the rock.

"Paddle back! Give it all you've got!" shouted Wild Wes. "Faster!"

I dug my oar into the water and pushed backward hard and fast. I could hear Mom behind me, out of breath, matching me stroke for stroke.

The distance to the rock shrank. The raft inched slightly right. But we weren't going to make it. I cut my eyes over at Stephanie and rowed harder.

"Paddle forward!" Wes shouted. "Get ready to ride the rapids, baby!"

Our raft missed the rock by inches, slid over a three-foot waterfall and into the boiling white water. Water cascaded over the sides of the raft, completely soaking us all. For a minute I thought we were going to flip over, but then the raft flew up and forward and we were through it.

"Whoo-hoo!" I shouted. This was as much fun as jumping fences on horseback, like riding at a full gallop. Fantastic!

"Yee-hii!" Mom shouted behind me. "All right!"

"Yikes!" Norm yelped.

Stephanie screamed.

"Paddle forward, paddle forward!" shouted Wild Wes.

I leaned into the oar. Laughing my head off because this was so much fun. The roar of the water filled every space inside my head. I glanced at Stephanie, whose face was totally white. She'd stopped paddling.

"Paddle harder, don't stop!" Wild Wes yelled. We dodged another rock that jumped out on the left. Then Wes squeezed us through a two-foot chute into the shallows, and suddenly we were gliding through calm water, and the roar settled to a sound as soothing as wind chimes.

"Way to go," said Wes.

"Whew!" Norm said. "Everybody okay?"

"Great!" said Mom.

"That was awesome!" I said.

"Awesome." Stephanie managed a grin.

"Well, you've conquered your first class four," said Wes. "One more to go, about a mile down. Right now everybody can take it easy. It's deep and calm through here. You can jump in and swim if you want."

"Seriously?" I said. I gazed at the wooded riverbank sliding by.

"Sure."

"Won't the raft leave them behind?" Norm asked.

"Just hang on to the side. Or, if you let go, we can always come get you." Wes grinned wickedly. "Or we can leave you out here for the bears and coyotes."

Stephanie gasped.

"Kidding!" Wild Wes said. He scooped up a handful of water. Tossed it at Stephanie.

"Here I go!" I laid down my oar, stood on the edge of the raft, and dove in.

"No diving!" shouted Wes as the water closed over my head. I opened my eyes and saw two small fish suspended a foot in front of my face, with black spots by their eyes. I reached for them and they darted away, then I swam upward through angled cones of light filtering from the surface. Suspended mud made the river water seem silky and thick.

"Whoo-hooo!" Wild Wes yelled as my head broke the surface. And he leaped. A wall of water exploded as he did a cannonball right next to me. He jerked his head sideways as he surfaced, tossing the water from his dreadlocks. "*Never* dive into a river, girl. Always jump."

"Sorry." I grinned at him, then grabbed an outside handhold and felt the cool tug of the water as the raft moved through it.

"Shouldn't you be in the raft?" Norm asked Wild Wes.

"Just taking a little dip, back in a sec," said Wild Wes. He was doing the backstroke.

"It's okay, Norm, I can steer it," Mom said. "Diana, stay close to the raft now, all right, sweetie?"

"Come on in, Steph," I said. "The water's great." I could tell from the way Stephanie looked at me that she was dying to come in but was afraid. Stephanie was such a chicken it was hard to resist teasing her. "If you see a copperhead, you don't have to worry because they can't bite you while they're swimming."

"Diana!" Mom said sternly. "That's mean." Mom squeezed Stephanie's knee. "There aren't any snakes in there, Steph."

"Oh, I don't know about that," said Wild Wes as he climbed back in the raft.

"That's it. I'm not swimming," Stephanie said.

"Me, neither," said Norm. He had his hand over Stephanie's shoulder, holding firmly, but I saw Stephanie shrug his hand off.

Wild Wes reached down to me. His grip was wiry and strong as he pulled me over the side. Water sluiced from our bodies and streamed into the raft. Thin rivulets washed over the blue-green sea monster on Wes's arm.

"I love your tattoo," I said.

"Thanks." Wild Wes flexed his muscle, and the monster appeared to slither along his arm.

"Did it hurt?" Stephanie asked.

"Yes, ma'am, it sure did; hurt like a son of a gun. Don't ever do it." Wes settled onto the back of the raft and grabbed his oar.

"Don't worry," said Stephanie.

I reached for my oar. How much could it hurt? I had tried to get a tattoo last year, but Mom refused to sign the waiver. That made me so mad. Mom said as long as she refused to sign I couldn't get a tattoo until

I was eighteen. I used to think when I got to Florida Dad could sign. Just thinking about Dad now made my whole chest and neck feel hot. Dr. Shrink's Moronic Mood-o-Meter jumped from a five to a seven and then back again.

In the brief silence after that, I heard the faint sound of rapids ahead.

I glanced over at Norm and saw that he heard them, too. He wasn't his jovial self. Was Norm scared? That seemed weird.

"Second set of class four rapids up ahead," said Wes. "This one happens to be called Gator Guts."

"What?" I laughed.

"Why?" Stephanie sounded like she was going to gag.

"Don't know," Wes said. "Now, if you'll look up there, those high school kids are going to the left of the rocks. Big mistake. Guaranteed wipeout. The only way through these rapids is to stay to the right of the rocks and row like crazy."

I looked at the raft with the high school guys. So far ahead, it looked small, like a toy, bouncing over the waves. There was a huge rock in the center of the river with waterfalls on either side. The guys were going left. Their raft slid over the falls, then I heard yelling and saw heads and legs flailing. The raft popped into the air, totally empty.

"Told you," said Wes.

Norm breathed out. "Are you sure we should let these kids go over those falls?"

"Absolutely, I am the king of the river," Wild Wes said. Bared his teeth and growled. "Paddle forward!"

The rock grew as we slid toward it. I shoved my feet deeper into the crevice under the side, tensed my thighs, and dug my oar through the water. The tiny people ahead were swimming toward the loose raft. One person threw a leg over the side, but the three others were bobbing like little crazy people in the water.

"Right back!" Wes shouted.

I glanced at Stephanie. Oops. She was starting to cry.

"Don't cry!" I said. "Paddle!"

"Come on, come on, get out of our way," Wild Wes growled, watching the tiny flailing people. "Move it!" Wes shouted.

But one of the people ahead must have gotten hurt or got his leg stuck in some rocks because the people were still splashing around at the foot of the falls. The one person who had managed to get back onto the raft had it perched on a small, flat rock in the middle of the rapids and was leaning out, trying to help the others.

"They're in our way," Wes said. "We can't go down yet. We've gotta go over to the shore and wait." Wes guided us to the far right side of the river. Yellow-green branches of weeping willows hung over and brushed the surface, forming a feathery, shifting screen.

I reached up and clasped a whip-like weeping willow branch.

"No! Don't—" Wes started.

The next thing I knew, the raft swept under me. I did a back flip into the water. I heard Mom and Stephanie scream before I went under. Something slammed into my thigh. I felt rocks beneath me and tried to get my head above the waves. I sucked in a whole bunch of muddy-tasting water. Which way was up? Which way was air? *God help me!* I prayed. This is it, I thought. My foot slid between two rocks.

The current dragged the raft and yanked on my foot. My skin scraped against the rock. I gasped and gulped down gallons of water. My foot was at such a strange angle.

"Mom!" I tried to shout. A wave smacked me in the face and filled my mouth with water. I choked. I tried pulling my foot again. I heard splashing, a loud roaring in my head sounded like screams. Then strong arms were pulling at my shoulders, strong fingers grasped my ankle and released my foot from the rock. I grabbed and wrapped my arms around Mom, trying to hang on.

But when my eyes cleared of water I saw Mom

leaning out of the raft, reaching for me with a paddle, her face terrified. The person I was holding on to, the person I was practically strangling, was Norm.

"You're okay," he said, holding me. His arms were wrapped around me. The water wasn't that cold but his teeth were chattering. "I've got you. You're okay."

I was pulled and lifted into the raft at the same time, and I laid there, catching my breath, shaking all over. Mom sat next to me, stroking my arm, murmuring soothing things.

"That was pretty swift there, Norm," Wes said. "Having a swimmer just upriver of Gator Guts is not a good thing." Wes had banked the raft along the edge between a rock and massive tree root. "You okay there, little lady?" he asked. I nodded, "What I'd been about to say is don't ever grab something that's onshore while the raft is still moving!"

"Well, she's okay and that's what matters," Norm said. I could feel his solid warm hand still resting lightly on my shoulder.

My ankle was scraped and bleeding. A bad bruise was starting to throb on my thigh, but Mom said nothing was broken or sprained. The high school guys had finally cleared the rapids. Their raft was a tiny yellow dot disappearing around the river bend. Wes said it was time to go.

I took a deep breath and glanced at Stephanie.

"You okay?" Stephanie said.

I nodded and grinned. "Never grab on to anything onshore while the raft is still moving."

"Got it."

"And never try to stand up in the river!"

"Right."

"All paddle!" Wes yelled.

I leaned into my oar as the rock loomed, the size of an elephant this time.

"Right back! Right back!"

I paddled. I glanced at Mom, who still looked pale, but she raised her eyebrows, smiled, and showed me crossed fingers.

"Paddle harder, right!" Wes shouted. "Give it everything! Don't hold back!"

The rock was ten yards away. Steph was practically crying with the effort of the rowing.

"Come on, Stephanie," Norm yelled.

"Come on, Steph, you're doing great!" I shouted.

The rock was on us. We weren't going to make it.

"Shove your oars into the side of the rock and push the raft away," Wes yelled. "Now!"

Stephanie and Norm shoved their oars into the side of the rock with all their might. The raft slid three feet to the right and spun around, so we were poised backward above a five-foot drop into a boiling, roaring white pit. My brain sizzled. I thought my heart would explode.

And then, like going down an elevator, we dropped with a loud whoosh. Walls of water came from everywhere! Stephanie screamed.

"All paddle! All paddle!" shouted Wes.

The raft did a full three hundred sixty-degree turn. Boiling white water rocketed us into the surging current. We bumped through the rapids like a horse trotting over a gravel road. And with an amazing suddenness, the roar of the water quieted and the raft began to glide. No one had the energy to say a word. I sat in a stupor with my oar on my lap, waiting for my heart to slow down.

"Congratulations, folks," Wes said at last. "You've just survived and conquered Gator Guts, the toughest class four rapids on the Big Pigeon. Take-out is just ahead."

"Yeee-hiii!" Stephanie shouted.

Wild Wes stretched his arms over his head and yawned. On his bicep, the sea monster's scales glistened. "The king of the river welcomes tips from all survivors."

I breathed out and felt light-headed with relief and joy. The muscles in my legs and arms twitched. My ankle ached. Mom squeezed my shoulder.

I felt kind of self-conscious about Norm, since he'd sort of saved my life. I didn't look at him, but I smiled at Stephanie and trailed my fingers in the silky water.

18

STEPHANIE

On the way home from rafting, Diana sat with me in the backseat of the car, wrapped in wet towels, laughing and singing along with the radio. We found little bits of leaves and algae on each other's legs and peeled them off and threw them in each other's hair. Daddy and Lynn were imitating Wild Wes, and Lynn's hand was resting on the back of Daddy's neck.

"I didn't tell you this, Lynn, but I've decided I'm going to quit my job and become a river guide," Daddy was saying. "I realize 'Norm' doesn't have quite the same ring as Wild Wes, so I've been trying to come up with a good name. How about 'The Norminator'?"

"I would go back to the drawing board," Lynn said.

I rolled my eyes and tried not to smile, but imagining Daddy as a river guide was just too funny.

"What about 'Norman the Nasty'?" Daddy said.

"Ewww," Diana said.

"How about 'Stormin' Norman'?" suggested Lynn.

"Ooh, that's good," Daddy said, nodding. "But hasn't it been taken?"

"'Abnormal Norman'?" said Diana.

"Hey, watch that, it's supposed to be a name that inspires fear and respect." But Daddy seemed tickled that Diana was joining in. "Okay, well, we'll put the name aside for the time being. But what about the tattoo? Since I'm an accountant, what about, say, an adding machine?"

"Daddy!" I was working hard not to laugh. "That is so lame!"

"Well, it would be a really mean-looking one, with jagged numbers on it."

We were a few miles from the ranch and I was smiling, turning to Diana, thinking that this felt so fun, like a real family. My eyes swept the darkening woods beside us, and I saw a gray shadow sliding between trees. My gaze froze. I blinked. Another shadow. I grabbed Diana's hand and pointed. Two gray, hooded heads, pricked ears, and slanted yellow eyes glided beside our car, floating like ghosts. Her hand covered her mouth, and she turned in her seat.

"Hey!" she screeched. "The wolves, we see the wolves!"

"What?" Dad hit the brake and glanced back at us. "Where?"

We both leaned out the window, pointing. By that time the wolves had melted into the shadows, and there was nothing for Dad and Lynn to see.

"Oh my gosh, I can't believe it!" Diana said. We shared a look of relief and hope. Maybe, somehow, we could fix what we'd done.

The minute we got back to the ranch, Dad pulled into the parking lot beside the barn, and Diana and I ran inside, looking for Maggie. Cones of sunshine shone from the doorway into the dark, pungent center of the barn. We found Maggie in the office.

"We just saw the wolves!" Diana said. "When we were driving back from rafting. Stephanie and I looked over beside the car and saw them running through the woods."

"How far away?" Maggie asked, dropping her clipboard.

"No more than three miles from here," Dad said as he and Lynn ran into the barn. We described the area where we'd seen them.

"Doc and I just spent the day putting out humane traps around Morgan's place, plus we put up a bunch of signs. You're sure it was Waya and Oginali?" Maggie reached for her cell phone and flipped it open.

"Yeah," Diana nodded and glanced at me. "They had the long legs and their heads looked like they were wearing gray hoods."

"It wasn't dogs; it was the wolves. I know it," I said.

"Fantastic!" Maggie turned toward Daddy and Lynn. "Could you help us out, folks? Could Russell and Doc take one of the girls with them so she could show them right where she saw them? They've only got room for one in the truck. Doc will have his tranquilizer gun. It would be a help if they could show them the exact spot."

"Me!" said Diana, raising her hand. "I'll go."

"You mean now?" Lynn said.

"Daylight's fadin'," Maggie said. "Wolves sleep during the day, and they're most active at dawn and dusk. We've got about two and a half more hours before they vamoose." She dialed a number on her cell phone.

"Pleeeeeeease?" Diana begged.

"Well … ," Lynn said.

"Absolutely not," Daddy said. "There is no way we are going to let her go out tramping around the woods at dusk after two *wolves*."

My heart squeezed tight and I felt dizzy. *I* was the one who had seen the wolves.

Lynn glared at Daddy, then turned back to Maggie. "Diana can go, Maggie, but she'll have to be home by ten. Diana, you need to go back to the cabin and put on warmer clothes."

"You're letting Diana go?" Daddy stared at Lynn.

"Yes, I am." Lynn's lips were pressed together in a straight line.

As she was dialing Doc's number on her cell phone, Maggie told Diana she'd meet her by the front door of the lodge in fifteen minutes. We all headed back to the car.

I walked way ahead of everyone else. Daddy and Lynn were arguing about letting Diana go. Diana was skipping along beside Lynn.

What about me?

Back in the cabin, Daddy went in the bedroom and shut the door. I stood by the CD player, lining up the CD cases, listening while Lynn lectured Diana about being safe. Diana hugged her mom and said thanks, and I saw Lynn run her fingers through Diana's hair. Sometimes Mama did that to me.

All of a sudden, I felt really homesick.

I felt betrayed. I turned and stared at Diana, my arms crossed. She didn't even notice.

I thought we'd had a pact about the things that happened that night. Riding our bikes through the mountain woods, releasing the wolves, the way they'd jumped over our heads while we were watching at the stars, and now Diana was going with Russell and Doc to look for them while I got left behind!

I knew there was only room for one in the truck, and I was kind of scared to go, but still.

I stomped upstairs to the loft, but nobody even looked. I sat on the floor beside my bed, took my cell phone from my suitcase, and plugged it in. Mama had said only to use it in an emergency, but how could Mama be mad about hearing my voice?

I dialed and listened to the ringing. Mama loved to have people over. I pictured her out by the pool, maybe wearing her bathing suit with one of her short black cover-ups and high-heeled flip-flops, surrounded by lots of people, laughing. She might not even hear the phone ringing.

"Hello?"

"Mama?" I could hear splashing and people talking and laughing in the background. Mama was out by the pool. It was nice out there on summer nights. The air felt like velvet.

"Stephanie? Well, hey, Sugar."

"Hey, Mama. I just wanted to call and say hello."

"Well, hey yourself. We're having some drinks and hors d'oeuvres out here by the pool. It's such a pretty night. You having fun?"

"Yeah," I said in a small voice.

"What's wrong?"

"Nothing. So, who's there?"

"Matt is here, and he brought some friends from college and we're just visiting. Everyone asked about you."

"Tell Matt hey. Did anybody call me?"

"Oh, listen, the phone rang off the hook the first two days you were gone, all your little friends calling. Let's see, Katie, Jessica, and Lindsay."

"They did?" I felt warm and loved and really homesick all at the same time.

"I told them you'd be home Sunday. How are you and Daddy getting along?"

"Okay. He made me go riding." I instantly felt like I was tattling on Daddy. I picked at a piece of carpet beside my leg and it started to come unraveled. I wondered if any of Matt's friends were staying in my room.

"Don't let him make you do anything you don't want to do, Sugar. What about Lynn? Is she being sweet to you? And Diana?"

"Diana's a spoiled brat," I heard myself say. "Lynn's

okay. She's not as pretty as you." I felt heat rising to my face and knew I should stop myself saying this stuff, but for some reason I couldn't. "Diana does wild stuff and tries to get me in trouble with her."

"Is that right? She takes that mood medicine, and hasn't she had some discipline problems? I've been worried about you spending time with her. Let me talk to your father," Mama said. Then there was a loud splash and Mama squealed. "Hey, stop that! You got my invitations soakin' wet!" But I could hear the laughter in her voice.

"No," I said quickly. "Daddy's busy right now, and I better go."

"If you want me to call your daddy and straighten this out I will."

"No, never mind, Mama, everything's fine. I better go. Don't call Daddy, okay? I really don't want you to."

"You're sure, now?"

"Yeah. I'll see you this weekend."

"Okay, Sugar. We miss you."

"Me, too." When I hung up I felt even worse than I had before I called. A dozen carpet loops were popped loose in a line that led under my bed.

It sounded like everyone was really having fun out by the pool. If I was there I probably could have had

Katie over and maybe Mama would take me shopping again. I was sitting on the floor, picking at the rug when Diana came back upstairs to get a sweatshirt.

I just couldn't hold it in anymore.

"Why didn't you at least ask me if I wanted to go in the truck?"

Diana threw her hands up at the ceiling. "I didn't think you'd want to. They can only take one person, and it happened so fast."

I glared at her. I had a terrible stomachache. I had not given up on friendship with Diana, and I had felt like I'd really made progress the night we'd let the wolves go. Even though what we'd done was wrong, there had been bonds formed between us. But now it was like friendship had these unwritten rules of loyalty, and Diana didn't pay any attention to them. If you shared some really special experience, there was a bond between you. If someone told you a secret of theirs, you'd share one of yours. If someone did a nice thing for you, you tried to do something nice for them. I had a feeling if I did twenty nice things for Diana, it wouldn't make a bit of difference. Why couldn't Diana figure that stuff out? I wished I'd never followed her up the mountain.

"If I help get the wolves back, it will be like it never happened in the first place."

I stared at Diana. "But it did happen. And what about me? What about our friendship?"

Diana pulled the sweatshirt over her head. "What about it?"

Diana was acting like nothing at all had happened the other night! Normally if a snappy comeback popped into my head, I'd chicken out before I said it. Or, I came up with comebacks way too late, after people left the room or later that night lying in bed. But tonight, everything came spilling out. "You know what, I tried to be like a sister. I tried to be a friend. Daddy told me about your medicine and stuff, so I really, *really* tried. I mean, I covered up for you and everything. But no wonder you don't have any friends. All you do is hurt people. No wonder everyone avoids you. No wonder your own daddy doesn't answer your texts."

Diana's eyes got all glassy. "What are you talking about? You don't know anything about my dad."

"Yes, I do. Your mom told me you'd texted and called your dad but he hasn't answered."

"Mom has no idea how my dad feels and neither do you. And stop trying to steal my mom!"

"Steal your mom?"

"You're always acting like you're having these personal little conversations with her. You're not! Okay? Butt out of my life!" She clattered down the stairs. The door slammed behind her. I heard Lynn call after her to be careful. Then I heard Lynn knock on Dad's bedroom door and Daddy said "What?" in a mad voice.

Now look what had happened. Everybody was mad at everybody else.

19

DIANA

Doc's old green pickup jounced over roots, sank over ruts, and ground over gravel. I was wedged in the jump seat beside Russell. Maggie and Doc sat up front. Tree limbs scraped the doors and poked through the open windows.

I thought about the fight with Stephanie and chewed my fingernail until a little bloody piece of cuticle came off. Where the heck would Stephanie sit, anyway? The four of us were already stuffed into the cab like sardines.

My thigh was touching Russell's. When the truck went over ruts we sometimes jostled each other.

"How do you drive this thing? I mean, there's not even a road," I said to Doc as we bounced over a rock the size of a basketball.

"That's why they call them all-terrain vehicles," said Russell.

"Duh," I said, making a face at him.

"This clearing is as far as I can take the truck," Doc said. "We'll have to go the rest of the way on foot." He cut the engine. The truck was tilting at an angle. The door squeaked loudly as it fell open.

Maggie climbed out, tucking her gray braid under her hat. "Okay, Diana, lead us to the spot."

Doc went around the back of the truck and got out the dart gun. He dropped a clear baggie with extra darts in the front pocket of his faded flannel shirt. The yellow feathery ends of the darts looked like canary tails. "Here's the deal," Doc said. "If we find them, and if I get a shot, it takes five to ten minutes for the anesthesia to take effect. And during that time Waya or Oginali could probably run three miles. So, Russell and Diana, have you got on your running shoes?"

"Yeah," Russell said. His face looked excited. Expectant.

"But if you catch up to them, don't get too close,"

Doc said. "Once we shoot them there's no telling what they'll do. Lead on, Diana. Wasn't there a Greek goddess of the hunt named Diana?"

"That's right," said Maggie. "Diana, the Huntress."

I blushed. Diana the Huntress sounded pretty cool. Then I glanced at Russell, embarrassed. "Uh, whatever." But I took long-legged steps through the woods and imagined myself with a golden bow over my shoulder. A quiver of arrows on my back.

I'd seen the wolves just before a dense copse of trees with pear-shaped leaves. If Stephanie hadn't seen them too I might have thought I'd just seen shadows. Actually Stephanie had seen them first. If she hadn't seen them, I may not have seen them at all.

As I led the others uphill, I scanned the shifting bands of light slanting through the trees, weaving through tree trunks. Leaves swished as the four of us brushed by low-hanging limbs. Sticks on the ground popped and cracked as we zigzagged through the woods. A little brown rabbit raced away through underbrush, its white tail bobbing.

"Look, how cute," I said to Russell.

"Lunch for Waya," he said.

"Ugh!"

"I'm just saying. The nature of the beast."

"That's the truth," Maggie said. "You can't judge the

wolves for being what they are. People have always laid this whole evil thing onto the wolves, and it's totally a myth. Although, I do think that a lot of the old Cherokee stories give human characteristics to the wolves."

"Yeah, like in that story about the two wolves fighting," said Russell.

"What story?" I said.

"Tell it," said Doc.

Maggie took a breath, then started telling the story. "An old Cherokee said that a fight was going on inside him, and it was between two wolves. One wolf was evil. He was anger, jealousy, and lies. The other wolf was good. He was kindness, generosity, and truth. The old man said that same fight between the two wolves is going on inside every person."

I stopped and looked back at Maggie. "Which wolf wins?"

Maggie pointed to Russell. "He knows this story. He's heard it before."

I turned to Russell. "Which wolf wins?"

"The one you feed," said Russell.

"The one you feed," I repeated. I stopped and leaned my palm against a tree. The ridges of bark felt rough, and small pieces came off on my fingers. I knocked the bark from my hands, thinking about the wolves leaping to freedom in the cold moonlight. I replayed that awful cell phone conversation with Dad. I heard my own voice telling Stephanie to butt out of my life. Had I been feeding the wrong wolf? I blocked out everything else and let the sounds of wind swishing through the trees fill my mind. I decided Dr. Shrink's Moronic Mood-o-Meter was a six, but if I concentrated and took slow breaths, I could make it go down to a five.

We continued walking, all the time my eyes searching, until some time later when I leaned against another tree. With the back of my wrist, I wiped sweat from the damp hairs at my temples. I looked up at the sun sinking behind the trees. The canopy of branches grew darker. Birds cackled and chortled around me, like kids in class after you've said something stupid. I yanked off my left shoe and shook out a stick the size of a chicken bone that had been digging into the sole of my foot.

How many miles had we covered, threading through tree trunks, climbing over rocks, tangled roots, and underbrush? Five? Ten? My ankle was killing me.

"Time's running out," Doc said.

"Let's split up," Maggie said. "Doc and I will head to the top of the ridge for one last loop. Russell, you and Diana meet back at the truck at sunset.

Russell agreed. I was too tired to do anything except

nod. I watched Russell as he squatted at the base of a tree a few yards away.

I was pretty sure Russell had started wondering if I'd made up seeing the wolves. He probably thought I'd led them on a wild goose chase. What if I had? What if the shadows I'd seen in the woods had been only what Stephanie and I wanted to see? What if we had been hoping so much that we'd wished them into existence?

"That story Maggie told," I said to Russell. "About the wolves."

"Yeah?" Russell, who had been scanning the woods, cut his eyes at me and blinked. Would he forgive me if he knew I had let the wolves go?

"What that story means is that all of those evil and good qualities are inside each of us," I said. "And the wolf that wins, or the qualities that win, are the ones that we feed? The ones we let grow?"

"I guess," Russell said.

I thought about what Stephanie had said today. About me never being able to be a friend and about Dad not answering my texts. How could that be? He was my dad. He was supposed to love me no matter what. When I'd talked to him this morning it didn't seem like he loved me at all. And Mom, she was always supposed to pick me. No matter what. But Stephanie was prettier, she was sweeter, she didn't have to take pills to get through the day. Maybe Mom had already started liking her better.

I took a few deep breaths. I'd always thought that people just were who they were. But the Cherokee story made it sound like people had a choice.

Wolves didn't—couldn't—choose. When Stephanie and I put the log in their pen, the wolves had no choice but to leap to freedom and run away. It was their nature. Their instinct. When they got hungry, it was their nature and instinct to kill and eat that farmer's chickens.

People aren't animals. That's what the Cherokee story was saying. We have a choice. I stopped at the river's edge and grabbed onto a small twisted dogwood that arced over the water. "Russell," I said.

"Yeah?"

"Would you ever move back with your dad? I mean, if you got mad at Maggie, or you couldn't stand living there anymore?"

"I did go back there once."

"Really?"

"Yeah. One time last year I went to this friend's house and forgot to call Maggie and tell her where I was. We were playing basketball in his driveway with the floodlights on, and I lost track of time. So Maggie didn't know where I was until like eleven o'clock. She grounded me for two weeks, and I thought that was outrageous, so I went to my dad's. I was there like three days, and then I went back to Maggie's."

"Why'd you go back?"

"Dad's cooking sucked. Just kidding. I don't know. Ever since Mom died … sometimes I hate him." There was a silence. "It's like we remind each other."

I let that sink in for a minute, nodding my head. A few minutes later, I headed through the woods again, leaving Russell leaning against the tree, squinting at me. The sun edged lower, mingling in the branches of the trees. The trunks of the pines were thick and straight, a deep chocolate brown, while the other trunks were slender and mottled gray. Leaves rustled and sticks snapped under my feet. A shadow moved across my eyes, and I looked up and saw the serrated boomerang shape of a buzzard wheeling just above the treetops. Ahead on the ground was a nondescript ripple in the landscape. A wilted hump of dead leaves. Or bedraggled gray rags. I stopped.

I narrowed my eyes and hurried closer. It wasn't dead leaves. It moved slightly. My heart tightened into a knot.

Russell crashed through the underbrush behind me. I waved at him to be quiet. His footsteps stopped.

Now I could make out a gray snout and throat, a

hooded head, powerful shoulder, rib cage, haunches, and tail. It was Waya. She was stretched on the ground.

I stepped closer and glanced around for Oginali but didn't see her. Waya was panting. Something was wrong. I took one more step, and another.

"It's okay," I whispered. "I won't hurt you."

Waya's ear moved, as if to say, "I hear you." The panting stopped. Her rib cage rose up and down, ever so slightly.

I took a few steps closer. Russell moved past me, then began to talk softly to Waya. "Good girl, it's just me, Russell. How's the girl doing?"

Russell knelt beside her. He kept the soft talk going, a steady stream of comforting sounds. Waya opened her eye a tiny slit and closed it again. Her eye didn't look golden anymore, but dull, as if everything had drained out. I watched the small movements of her rib cage. A matted spot on Waya's shoulder looked dark and wet.

"Someone shot her," Russell said in a low voice.

Waya's rib cage stopped moving.

"Russell, she's stopped breathing!" Hot tears sprang to my eyes, and Waya and the trees went out of focus. Waya was dying! Guilt hit me like a wave, breaking over my shoulders. "This is my fault," I said.

"It's not your fault," said Russell. He didn't even look

up at me. He touched Waya's flank with a steady, gentle hand. Waya whined, but it was faint, as if she were already going away.

"I'm the one who let her go!" Words and tears streamed out together. "Stephanie and I, three nights ago. We didn't know this would happen. I would never hurt her on purpose, never in a million years."

Now Russell did look at me. I never wanted to see a look like that again. And now Maggie would look at me like that, too. And Doc. And Norm. And even Mom.

"Go find Doc and Maggie," Russell ordered. "I'll stay here with her."

I turned and ran.

20

STEPHANIE

Nick had been kneeling at the edge of the pond, baiting hooks on two bamboo poles with bologna. When I told him about the wolves, he stopped and stared at me with his mouth hanging open.

"You're kidding!" Nick said. "Everyone's been spending all this time looking for them and y'all haven't said anything?"

"Stop looking at me like that!" I said, and I grabbed one of the poles. Without my usual caution, I tossed the bologna in the water, then watched the greasy quarter-sized rainbow that formed where the bologna sank. I'd thought it would be such a relief to tell someone, but I didn't feel any better, the way he looked at me.

I wished I hadn't said those things to Mama about Diana earlier tonight. I didn't like what Mama said about Diana being on medicine and having problems and not wanting me to spend time with her. Mama didn't even know Diana.

I threw a pebble in the pond and watched the widening circle of ripples move outward. I'd read in my science book this year that a tsunami was like a gigantic version of a pebble being thrown in a pond. Underwater earthquakes radiated energy that moved five hundred miles per hour through the water and crashed on beaches thousands of miles away.

"If we could just find them, everything would be okay." This was exactly what Diana had said after dinner, and I hadn't believed her, but now here I was saying it to Nick.

Nick shrugged, as if realizing this had nothing to do with him. "Maybe they'll luck out."

"Maybe." I stared at the fading light reflected on the surface of the pond. "You and I could go look for 'em," I added.

"Yeah, right." Nick threw his line in the water. Now he wasn't looking at me at all.

I watched his bologna sink. "Hey, I'm serious; why couldn't we? Maggie said they set traps around Mr. Morgan's place. We could check and see if they came back, try to find 'em before Mr. Morgan does."

"It's gonna be dark in an hour, and how are we supposed to catch them? Put a leash on them? They're practically wild."

"I don't know. We could figure that out if we see them." He faced me again, and I looked at his light brown freckles. He looked like a little kid with those freckles, young and innocent. "Please?" I asked. "I feel horrible, and I want to try to fix it. We could take the bikes, just like Diana and I did."

A few minutes later we were bouncing on bicycles through the woods over rutted, hard-packed bridle trails. I couldn't remember which trail I'd been on when I'd gone riding, or how we found the pen before. But since it wasn't dark yet, the sound of the wind through the trees was soothing and not scary. The birdcalls and scurrying animals didn't give me goose bumps. When we came to a fork in the path, I had no idea which way to go.

"What do you think?" Nick straddled his bike and peered down both ways. Now that he'd agreed to come along with me, he seemed more like his old self.

"No clue," I said. I stopped and fished in my pocket for a ponytail holder and twisted it around my hair. "But I think we should keep going uphill."

We picked the left fork and kept climbing the mountain until we came to trails that were so steep we had to get off and walk the bikes. Were these the same trails I'd been on with Diana a few nights ago? I couldn't remember, but they didn't seem familiar.

"Maybe we should leave the bikes here," I said, leaning into the handlebars and gasping for breath. My lungs were screaming for air.

Then I looked up and saw the rock face Diana and I had climbed. The other night it had seemed like some awful evil crag. In the rosy light of sunset, it looked smaller, and it was easy to see places to put your hands and feet.

"The wolf pen is right at the top of this rock," I said. "I bet we're on Mr. Morgan's property now." A shiver ran across the back of my neck.

Nick looked at the cliff face. "Hey, at least we get to practice our rock climbing," he said. "But if you fall, it's adios, amigo."

"Yeah." I leaned the bike against a tree and stood at the foot of the rock with my hands on my hips. I remembered how cold and scared I'd been that night, my flip-flops sliding on the dark rock face, scraping my bare toes. I was still scared, but now something new was happening. I kept going anyway.

I pulled myself up to a small shelf that had been invisible a few nights ago. I leaned close to the wall and edged my way over to a place where there was a root hanging over the rock top. I grabbed the root, wedged my toes onto a small outcropping, and with all my strength, pulled myself up and over the edge. I lay with my feet dangling, catching my breath, and glanced down at Nick, ten feet below, watching me. One of the rhinestones from my jeans fell down the rock face, sparkling as it bounced. Looking down made me light-headed, so I turned around. I shimmied onto the ground above the rock, grabbed the chain-link fence, and was finally able to stand up.

"I made it. Come on up," I called.

Since Nick was taller, climbing was easier for him, and he was lying on his stomach beside me in just a couple of minutes. Keeping the fingers of one hand wrapped around the cage fence, I offered him my other hand. He took hold, and I pulled him up the last two feet.

"Whew!" I said once we were both standing on the ledge. We edged our way up to the gate, holding on to the fence. It squeaked as we climbed. Finally, we reached level ground.

"I can't believe you guys did this in the dark," said Nick. "I mean, look down there. Heart attack city, man."

"I can't look," I said. I looked over to where Diana and I had slid the dead tree over the fence. Someone, probably Russell, had pulled it down and it was lying inside the pen. The gate was double-locked the same as before.

"Now what?" said Nick.

"I guess we look for the traps," I said.

"My dad says they normally cover traps with leaves and stuff, so be careful." Nick caught my eye, then ducked his head. "Maybe grab a stick and use it to feel the ground in front of you."

"Good idea." I poked around until I found a stout stick and brandished it like a cane as I crashed through the woods. Nick and I stuck together at first and then split up, winding through clusters of trees and wading through fallen leaves, vines, and underbrush. The last purple light before dusk filtered through the green veil of branches. Cool air brushed my arms. It would be dark soon.

I stopped on a high slope, looked down, and saw the lodge, sort of snuggled into the meadow. Dirt roads looked like thin red lines crisscrossing the stands of trees on the mountainside, like places where a wound had been stitched up.

I was out of breath and could feel the blood pumping next to my collarbone.

Doc had described the traps as "padded leghold traps," which would trap an animal's leg but not break the skin. But he said they had to be checked a lot because sometimes an animal would injure itself trying to escape, or even chew off its own foot to get free. And what would I do if I found Waya or Oginali in one of those traps? They would surely try to bite me.

The sky above the lodge was still really bright, but the woods were dimmer now. Nick headed farther away. Leaves rustled and pine needles whispered as he walked.

And then it happened. The moment my foot landed, I knew it wasn't the ground. I tried to jerk my foot away but it was too late.

Thwack! The trap slammed shut just above my ankle.

The pain was awful. I screamed and fell backward.

"Nick!"

I sat up and tried to wedge my fingers under the steel rods clamped together over my leg. From that spot pain spread out in all directions.

Nick was crashing through the woods, and now he was beside me, kneeling. "Oh, man!"

I thought I might faint. "Get it off of me!"

"Okay, okay, give me a minute."

He ran his hand through his hair and looked around like he might find a key or something. I started crying and turned my face toward a tree. I felt his fingers gripping and pulling, but I couldn't look. Bolts of pain shot up to my waist. I tried to relax my muscles, and it did help a little. "Good thing there aren't teeth. And you have on jeans. Maybe if you took off your boot and just left it in the trap."

"Just get it off, please!" I couldn't think about anything but the pain.

"Maybe there's a release lever," he said. A minute later he pressed something, the steel bars opened, and the pain went away. I writhed away from the trap, pulling my leg free, and lay on the ground, breathing hard.

"I'm scared to look at it," I said. But I had to.

I sat up, dragged both palms across my face, and then pulled up the cuff of my jean.

It was getting dark and hard to see. I ran my hands over my ankle but felt no blood. The side of my ankle was the size of a golf ball, and my shin bone was swollen and tender to the touch.

Then, close by, a dead branch snapped. Nick and I both looked up and saw somebody's shadow framed against the sunset.

"Hey!" Nick shouted.

I heard myself scream.

"I figured it was you kids that done this." It was Mr. Morgan's raspy voice.

I thought my heart would jump right out of my throat.

"Hey, we're not doing anything." Nick's voice was shaking, higher than usual, and he stood up. "We just wanted to see if we could find the wolves. We didn't hurt anybody."

"We're just trying to get your wolves back." I heard a brave-sounding voice and was amazed to realize it was my very own.

"Shut up!" Mr. Morgan snapped. "If I'd talked to my father like that he'd have knocked me cold."

"Please, Mr. Morgan. I promise you, we're trying to get your wolves back."

"Ever occur to you that you might be trespassin'?"

What would he do to us? Mr. Morgan's hair looked wild and uncombed and there was a sweetish smell coming from him that I remembered from a man downtown who asked Mama for money once. Mama said he was drunk.

"We didn't mean to trespass," I said in a small voice.

"No back talk! I'm takin' you to my cabin. Now move!"

Mr. Morgan gestured for us to walk ahead of him toward his cabin. I stayed close to Nick, and he held my arm as I limped along. My mouth had gone completely dry and my knees were nearly buckling under me. I knew there was dirt everywhere on me. Suddenly I desperately wanted a shower. We headed real slowly toward the dark cabin in the woods. All we heard was our own breath and Mr. Morgan's boots crashing in the underbrush behind us.

I whispered prayers to myself. *Dear God, please help me be brave again.*

Just barely turning my head, I sneaked a look toward the lodge. It looked so sweet, like a doll house or something, with its green roof, gray-white smoke curling from the chimneys, and golden squares of light shining from the dining room windows. The sloping pasture, dotted with yellow flowers and salt licks, darkened as the sun dropped lower. The scene was so peaceful. I wiped both cheeks with my sleeve.

I imagined Mr. Morgan's hand touching my shoulder. My skin crawled at the thought of it.

Then I saw Doc's green truck, like one of those matchbox toys, kicking up a red swirl of dust as it climbed a nearby hill. From this distance the dirt road looked like an orange strand of yarn. Russell was riding in the truck bed, leaning over something. Was that one of the wolves?

I drew in my breath and glanced away, so that Mr. Morgan wouldn't see. But it was too late.

"What're you looking at?" Morgan stopped and squinted across the chasm down at the truck climbing the hill. "Is that one of my wolves?"

21

DIANA

I jumped out when Doc pulled his truck into a lot beside a converted barn. A weathered wooden sign outside said **MOUNTAIN MIST COMPANION HOSPITAL**. Doc lowered the truck gate and tossed his keys to Maggie, who ran to unlock the door.

Russell, kneeling in the truck bed, slid the stretcher toward Doc.

"Easy," said Doc. "As easy as you can."

Waya looked dead. A lot of the fur on her stomach was dark and wet with blood.

Together, Russell and Doc carried Waya into the hospital while Maggie held open the door. I followed behind, feeling guilty and useless.

Inside was a small waiting room with old wooden chairs and a linoleum floor. A counter divided the room. Behind it was a wall of files and a bookcase crammed with thick textbooks and dusty diplomas propped on top. On the counter was a ceramic statue of a smiling golden retriever standing up on his hind legs, wearing a white coat and stethoscope, and holding a large syringe. The caption said, "Paybacks are hell."

"Keep going straight back to the OR," Doc instructed Russell.

Maggie turned on the lights in Doc's operating room, and on Doc's orders, lay towels on the metal operating table in the center of the room. Doc and Russell lifted Waya onto the table.

"Grab that IV stand over there, please, Diana," Doc said. He lathered his hands and arms over a deep sink.

This was the first time anyone had said anything to me since I'd told Russell about letting the wolves go. I got the feeling that if they could have thrown me out of the moving truck they would have. As quickly as I could, I pulled a metal stand on wheels over next to the operating table.

"Now, I need all three of you to lift her up so I can

get this compression bandage around that wound to stop the bleeding."

"On three," said Maggie. "One, two, three." We raised Waya up. My arms shook, but I didn't let Waya's hind section drop. Doc tightly wrapped a bandage around her abdomen.

"Okay, lay her down now. I don't know if I can reach any of my assistants this time of night. You folks might have to help me do surgery," Doc said.

A spot on the bandage started to turn pink.

"Let's get a muzzle on her. She'll bite if she's scared. Diana, there's one in the bottom drawer over there."

I found the leather muzzle. I hoped Doc wouldn't ask me to put it on Waya.

Doc took the muzzle from me and slid it over Waya's jaws, then buckled it behind her head, all the while talking to her. Waya moaned softly.

"We need blankets," Doc added. "Check the closet in the hall."

I ran down the hallway, opening doors until I found the linen closet. I bundled several blankets in my arms and rushed them back.

Maggie and Russell gently spread them over Waya.

"Maggie, you and Russell hold her while I get the IV going," Doc instructed. And then he began shaving the fur from the top of Waya's front leg.

My eyes burned, and my throat caught so I couldn't breathe for a moment. I stroked Waya's ears and pulled my hand back when I felt the heat of Russell's eyes.

Doc hung a bag of clear liquid on the IV stand, swabbed brown, sharp-smelling iodine on the bare patch on Waya's leg, and used what looked like a long needle to start the IV.

"I'm letting the fluids run in full blast," he said.

Now he examined Waya, shining a penlight in her eyes. Lightly pressing on the bandage, which had stained a deep red. He lifted the skin of her snout, revealing her sharp teeth, and then pressed on her gums with the ball of his thumb. "Don't like her color," he said.

"She gonna make it, Doc?" Russell whispered.

"Too soon to tell." Doc clicked off the penlight. "She looks like she's in shock. I want to get at least one bag of fluids in her before I try to get that bullet out."

"Please save her," I said, practically choking.

"You know what?" Russell said. He finally looked at me, the pupils of his eyes huge with anger. "She could die. And it would be—"

"Russell!" Maggie cut him off. "Shhh! What we need to do right now is help Waya."

Doc was making calls to see if he could get some assistance. I heard a dog barking back in the kennel area. Its voice sounded hoarse and lonely.

"Nobody's home." Doc left messages for both of his assistants and hung up. He yanked the rubber band from his gray-blonde ponytail, shook his hair out. Pulled it back again, tighter this time. "As soon as I can get this bolus into her, I'm going to need some help with surgery."

"How long?" Maggie asked.

"It'll take about fifteen minutes for the fluid to run, and then the surgery itself will take about two hours."

Maggie looked at her watch. "I can't! I've got desk duty at the lodge tonight. I already took one day off this week." Maggie patted Russell's shoulder. "You're gonna have to help Doc do this, Russell."

Russell nodded.

I swallowed and looked only at Doc. "I'll help," I said.

Doc nodded. Five minutes later, Maggie left in the truck. I didn't dare try to talk to Russell. It was pretty clear he wanted nothing to do with me. It was as though all we'd talked about that first night, all we'd shared today had never happened. We sat in silence watching the level in the bag of fluid drop and the stains on Waya's bandage grow.

Suddenly a truck screeched to a halt outside.

"Did Maggie forget something?" Doc came back from prepping for surgery. He wore a green gown and rubber gloves.

The front door slammed and someone shouted, "Doc! I know you're in there!"

I glanced at Russell, who sat bolt upright.

"My dad!"

Just then Stephanie and Nick showed up at the end of the hall. Their faces looked white. Stephanie was limping. Joe Morgan stepped around the corner behind them. "Go on," he said, pushing them forward. "Look who I found by my wolf pen."

I stared at Stephanie, who saw Waya lying on the surgical table and covered her mouth with her hand.

Mr. Morgan saw, too, and his face flushed. "What have you done to her?"

"Someone shot her, Joe," said Doc carefully. "I'm getting ready to remove the bullet so I can try to save her."

"You got no right to do this without my permission."

"Dad!" Russell jumped up. "You can't just let her die!"

"It ain't my fault she's shot. These here kids admitted to letting my wolves go."

"You have to let Doc save her life," I said.

"Yeah? And who's gonna pay for it? You?"

Russell's voice was monotone when he spoke. "If you let her die, Dad, I'll never forgive you. Not ever. Not for the rest of my life."

"You ain't never gonna forgive me anyway, so what's the difference?" Mr. Morgan whispered.

There was a horrible silence, and the air closed so tightly around us I could hardly breathe. Stephanie drew in her breath, and I looked over at her. We both knew Russell and his dad weren't talking about Waya now.

And I suddenly realized how Russell's mom had died. Russell's dad had been driving the car. Stephanie's face showed recognition, too.

"Hey," Doc said. "I'm not even—"

"I'll pay for it," I interrupted. "I've saved two hundred dollars. And if it's more I'll send my allowance every week. Whatever it costs. This was my fault. Not Stephanie's or Nick's."

Mr. Morgan glanced at me. The whites around his small brown eyes were tinged with red. He rubbed his cheeks, then shrugged and said, "Go 'head." He seemed much smaller now. He stared at Stephanie and Nick and then turned to leave.

"I'll see they get back to the lodge later," Doc said, and then returned to the operating room.

Stephanie and Nick clearly looked relieved.

Mr. Morgan looked at Russell, and after a long minute, he heaved a sigh and shuffled down the hall. A moment later the door slammed and his truck started.

I looked at Russell. His face was wet. He turned away from me.

Doc called us from the surgery room. "Russell! Diana, her color is coming back. Time to work."

We hurried in as Doc turned on the anesthesia machine and held a mask over Waya's muzzled snout. After a few minutes, he took the muzzle off. Her jaw hung open limply.

"Put your hands under her body and help me roll her over onto her chest."

Russell and I rolled Waya up on her chest. Stephanie and Nick stood in the doorway and watched.

"I need one of you to open her jaw while I pass a tube into her windpipe. Just spread her jaws wide open."

Russell didn't hesitate. He hooked his fingers over the ends of her teeth and opened her mouth wide, revealing her grayish-pink tongue lolling between yellow fangs.

"Good work." Doc pulled her tongue forward, then slid a clear plastic tube down her windpipe. He hooked the tube to the anesthesia machine.

We helped Doc roll her again, onto her back this time. The green line on the blipping monitor told us Waya's heart was beating, but she seemed totally lifeless. Doc clipped the fur on her abdomen and around the bullet wound and swabbed the whole area with iodine.

He tossed surgical masks to Russell and me. "Put

these on," he said. He soaped his hands up to the elbows and put on a green surgical cap, mask, and plastic gloves.

With shaking hands, I tied on the mask.

I looked at Russell. Above his mask, the whites of his eyes showed all the way around.

Doc unrolled a couple of surgical packs on a tray, pulled up a stool, and selected a scalpel. Then he cut a long incision right down the middle of Waya's belly.

Dark blood oozed out. I glanced at Russell. His eyes looked scared above the green of his mask.

Doc inserted a metal retractor into the abdomen to hold the incision apart and suctioned out some blood.

Doc examined Waya's abdomen. "Looks like the bullet destroyed part of the spleen," he said. "I've got a spurter in here. I need one of you to wash your hands and throw on a pair of surgical gloves."

"I will," said Russell. He washed his hands and then got a pair of rubber gloves from the same box Doc used. They snapped as he pulled them on.

"Have a spleen," Doc said, holding up a purplish-red organ shaped like a big tongue. "Hold it while I tie off the vessels."

Because Doc was so sure and calm about what he was doing, I felt calm, too. I looked at the spleen with curiosity and fascination.

Doc placed Waya's spleen in Russell's outstretched hand and began tying knots around the vessels attached to it. Suddenly Russell swayed.

"Oops," said Doc. "You're looking green around the gills, buddy."

I glanced at Russell's face, which had gone pale. He dropped the spleen back inside Waya.

"Russell!" barked Doc. "Diana, walk him out into the hall!"

I grabbed Russell's arms. His weight was starting to sink onto me when I got him into the hallway. I felt strangely detached as I watched Nick and Stephanie help him slide down the wall.

"Get back in here, Diana, I need you!"

I ran back.

"Quick, I've got a gusher; wash up and get on a pair of gloves!"

I somehow managed to wash my hands and get the gloves on, but it was like I was outside my body, dimly aware of what I was doing. Then I was standing above Waya, my palms opened, and Doc gave me Waya's spleen. I watched a pulsing blood vessel attached to the spleen as it pumped blood into the open belly.

Doc quickly clipped a pair of scissors around the bleeder, only it had serrated teeth like a steak knife and clasped instead of cut. "Got it," he said. "Now I need another pair of hands."

"Steph!" I yelled. "Doc needs you!"

Stephanie limped up behind me.

"Grab that hemostat!" Doc yelled. "Those angled scissors!"

Her eyes went wide, but she limped over to the operating table and held the hemostat in both hands.

"Just like that. Don't move until I say so." Doc used surgical thread to tie knots around the blood vessels leading to the spleen. "I'm tying off the blood vessels so I can remove the spleen and stop the bleeding," he said. My shoulders were beginning to cramp from holding my hands so still. A spot between my eyes itched, but I dared not move. Stephanie was gripping the hemostat with both hands and blowing upward at stray hairs in the corners of her eyes.

"One spleen," said Doc, taking the spleen from me.

"She doesn't need it?" I asked, letting my shoulders relax.

"She can live without it." Doc examined the injured organ. "Well, good news and bad news. The good news is the hemorrhaging has stopped. The bad news is I can't find the bullet. It's still somewhere inside."

"Oh, no," I said, feeling panic rising again.

Doc placed the damaged spleen on a tray and gently, patiently searched inside Waya for what seemed like an endless period of time. My chest started to hurt. I realized I'd been holding my breath. I let it out slowly, watching Waya's heartbeat on the monitor.

"If I can't find it, we'll have to take an X-ray," whispered Doc under his breath. More seconds ticked by, then he sharply inhaled. "Got it!" Doc held up a mangled gold pellet. "Hey, it's scrunched. It was underneath the kidney, right up against her aorta. She is one lucky wolf. Waya, you put a hurting on this bullet, didn't you, girl?"

I stared at the squashed bullet. I could not believe that such a small thing had done such horrible damage to Waya's insides.

"We can close," said Doc. His voice sounded almost happy. "It's still very much touch and go, but you've done a good job, Diana. You, too, Stephanie."

I breathed while Doc sutured the bullet hole and incision and then bandaged Waya, and Stephanie and I followed his instructions to get a cage ready. He turned off the gas machine and removed the tube from the wolf's windpipe. Waya started to whimper.

I passed Russell and Nick in the hall, my arms full of clean towels. Russell stood up, looking embarrassed. "Is she gonna live?" he asked.

His voice had lost some of its harsh tone, and I felt my chest loosen a tiny bit more. "Doc says it's touch and go," I said. "Do you want to go back in?"

"Nah," Russell said. "Not right now."

But Nick went into the operating room and helped carry Waya to the recovery room. He gently laid her on the folded towels. Doc attached her IV bag to the metal door of the cage. He stood looking at Waya through the kennel walls.

"Doc," Nick said in a low, questioning voice. "Uh, Stephanie stepped into a trap. Could you take a look?"

"Sure," Doc said. "We might need to go down the mountain to the emergency room."

While Doc looked at Stephanie's leg, I stroked Waya's head as gently as I could, with only the backs of my fingertips, and talked softly to her. I had wanted freedom for Waya. Instead I landed her in this cage, barely able to move.

"You're lucky," Doc said while holding Stephanie's foot. "You're able to put weight on it, so I'm pretty sure it's just a bad bruise. Definitely have it checked out, though." He lowered her foot and reached into his pocket. "By the way, Diana," he added. "Here's a souvenir for you." He placed the small, misshapen bullet into my waiting palm.

22

STEPHANIE

"**W**hat were you *thinking*?" Daddy yelled.

I scooted closer to Diana on the couch. Now that it was us against Daddy and Lynn, all of a sudden all those things we'd said to each other earlier tonight didn't seem so important.

It was way past midnight. Diana and I had mud caked around the calves of our jeans, leaves in our hair, and blood smeared all over our T-shirts.

Dad's ears were as red as a neon Bojangles sign. Lynn's lips were a thin line and her arms were crossed tightly across her chest, almost as if she had to hold them there.

"You know," said Lynn in a measured tone, "I can understand your humanitarian interest in freeing the wolves. I can see how you'd truly be thinking you were doing a good thing. But lying about it for three days!"

"Out there wandering around the woods in the dead of night! Do you have any idea how dangerous that was?" Daddy yelled. "One or both of you could've fallen halfway down the mountain and been seriously injured! Stephanie, what if that trap had been a different kind?"

"Norm, you're yelling," Lynn said.

"Of course I'm yelling!" Daddy yelled. "That's what people do when they get angry!" But then he took a deep, slow breath and walked in a circle around the room with his hands in his pockets.

"It was my fault," Diana said in a quiet, even voice. "It was my idea, and Stephanie followed me. So you can blame me."

My heart went crazy and I got this big old lump in my throat. Diana was taking the blame!

"Don't worry, young lady!" Lynn said. "I've lived with you for fourteen years. This little scheme has *Diana* written all over it! And I even covered for you without knowing it!"

There was no way I was going to let Diana do this.

"I made my own choice to go," I said. I cut my eyes over to Diana. "And we did our best to fix what we'd done."

There was a dark sort of silence, since nobody had seen hide nor hair of Oginali since the wolves had been let go. We all took a minute to think about where Oginali might be now. Maybe lying injured somewhere. Maybe dead.

"What were you *thinking*?" Daddy said again, but a little bit more quietly this time. He sat down in an easy chair and stared first at me, then at Diana. "I guess I can give you credit for trying to make things right once you realized that what you did was wrong," he said. "There are lots of consequences to this. When I talked to Mr. Morgan, he said you had agreed to pay for Waya's surgery. I can't argue with him. You are responsible. Mr. Morgan will most likely want to be compensated for the loss of that other wolf. How do you girls plan to come up with that money?" He exchanged a look with Lynn.

"I have two hundred dollars saved," said Diana. "The money I was going to use to buy a horse."

"I have a hundred," I said. I'd planned on buying art supplies and speakers for my room, but it looked like that would have to wait.

"If it's more, we could pay Doc from our allowance," Diana suggested. "Until it's paid."

"All right then." Daddy let out a long exhale. "On our way out of town Saturday, we'll stop by Doc's office, and you two can talk to him about paying for the surgery." He took another deep breath and slapped his knees like he just realized something. He turned to Lynn and asked, "What exactly did you mean when you said you covered for Diana?"

Lynn didn't look so good. I felt real sorry for her. She had been trying to help Diana. I held my breath. Would she tell Daddy about the lie she told?

"I lied to you, Norm. About Diana. She'd gone riding the morning after you grounded her from the barn. I knew it, and I didn't tell you."

Dad's face was suddenly sad. "You lied to me? How can you yell at the kids for lying when you lied to *me*?"

"Listen, I know it was wrong. I know Diana was disrespectful. She was. But you were out of line, too, disciplining her like that without talking to me first." Lynn watched her own hands as she twisted her new wedding ring around her finger. "I love you, Norm, but Diana is my only child. No one will ever, ever take her place."

I felt movement beside me and saw Diana duck her head and scrub tears from her cheeks with the end of her sweatshirt. I felt so emotional. I wanted to give her a big old hug, and I knew she didn't like hugging all that much, but I decided to anyway. But then she leaned toward me and grabbed my shoulders with this really tight grip that surprised tears into my eyes. And then we all started bawling like little babies.

"Well," said Lynn, blowing her nose. "I guess we're really a family now, since we're all crying!"

* * *

The next morning I put on my crummiest clothes and went down to the barn by myself. I found Maggie there in the office and I said, "I feel really bad for what we did. Can I help out in the barn, like you said?"

Maggie looked at me with flat-looking eyes, and at first I thought she was going to send me away. But then she led me to the tack room. She handed me a pair of heavy gloves and a shovel and put me to work mucking stalls. Honestly, it was disgusting. It got all over my clothes, it smelled awful, and flies crawled on me and buzzed around my ears. My leg was killing me. After about an hour of scooping poop, the morning trail ride came in and Maggie handed me a curry brush and introduced me to Sam. I spent another hour currying Sam and cleaning his hooves. At first my hands shook, my leg ached, and my heart was just pounding. But the minutes went by, and Sam's tail swished in a real contented rhythm, like the metronome when I practiced my piano. I got more used to Sam, and Sam got more used to me, and bit by bit I calmed down.

I was determined not to quit the barn chores until Maggie said I was done. By late afternoon I pretty much thought I would be sleeping in the barn that night, but Maggie finally appeared.

"Hey, Sam, Stephanie's got you looking pretty good, hasn't she?" Maggie smacked Sam's butt and smoothed her hand over his neck. "Miss Stephanie, you done good. I happen to know a lot of wolf stories. I told Diana one. How would you like to hear one about a maiden who went out into the woods and met a wolf with his leg in a trap?"

My calf flinched just at the mention of a trap. "Sure," I said, pushing my hair out of my eyes with the back of my hand.

"The wolf said to the maiden, 'Please let me go.'

And she said, 'If I release you, how do I know you won't kill me?'

And the wolf said, 'You'll just have to trust me.'

So the maiden released the wolf.

Afterward, he said, 'Thank you, kind maiden.' He plucked a lash from his eye, gave it to her, and He said, 'Use this, and be wise. From now on you will look through my eyes, and you will see clearly.'"

On the way back to the lodge I thought about what

the story meant. Nick was playing basketball by himself at the half-court across from the lodge.

"Hey," he said. He wiped his forehead with his shirttail. His T-shirt was drenched with sweat. He stepped closer, arms open. "Want a hug?" he asked.

I laughed and opened my arms. "Sure. I've been at the barn mucking stalls."

Nick stepped away. "Maybe we can hug ... after respective showers, if you know what I mean. How's the leg?"

"Just bruised. Doc and Lynn both looked at it and said nothing's broken or sprained. I should be okay in a few days."

"That's a relief." He picked up the basketball, bounced it twice, then looked away. "Hey, last night was pretty wild, huh? I can't say I ever expected to be watching surgery in the middle of the night. It was cool."

"Yeah. I was surprised myself." Surprised *at* myself, I thought.

"I have your number so we can text. And this fall when we play you guys in soccer, maybe you could come over to my side of the field and say hey."

"Sounds good to me." I smiled. "Hey, let's hug now. I can handle it if you can."

And so we did. He felt warm and kind of damp, and my ear was right against his heart and it was beating really hard. So was mine.

* * *

I pulled myself up onto the top rung of the barn fence beside Diana. I waved at Nick, who was leaning against the fence a few feet down. He looked cute. His hair was slicked back, and he was wearing brand new cowboy boots. I could have told him that old grubby ones were better.

The sun was coming up, chasing away the puffs of morning fog hugging the mountain slopes around us. Inside the barn, a horse whinnied in what I now knew was a friendly way.

"You lost another rhinestone," Diana said, pointing to my jeans.

"Oh well." I watched the barn hands bring out the horses. "Are you ridin' Copper in the rodeo?"

"I better be." But Diana grinned when she said it.

"I'm riding Sam."

"He's a good horse for you. He's big but very gentle." Diana pulled something out of her pocket and held it out for me. "Here. Give this to Sam and he'll love you forever."

I held out my palm, and Diana gave me a sugar cube. "Thanks," I said.

"How's your leg?" Diana asked.

"It hurts, but not as much as yesterday. What about yours?"

"It hurts, but not as much as yesterday."

We both kind of laughed. I blinked and scanned the mountain ridge behind the barn. "Wonder where Oginali is right now," I said. "I wish we could have found her."

"She must be so scared," said Diana. "I feel so sorry for her."

"Me, too." I looked at Diana and realized that the wolves were almost like people to her.

"I heard Russell went out looking for her again last night, back around where we found Waya." Diana picked at a splinter on top of the rail fence and wouldn't meet my eyes. "You know, when I first saw the wolves, I thought I was more like Waya, and I hated Oginali."

"Hated her?"

"I thought she was weak. But I don't know. She may not be as brave as Waya, but she's so loyal it really touches me."

To me, they were just two wild animals. But it felt good that Diana was talking to me like this.

"Listen," I said. "I'm real sorry about what I said about your dad. I shouldn't have said that."

Diana watched the horses for a minute. "It's okay."

"But your dad *should* write or call you back."

"My brain knows that. My heart is having a little more trouble with it. But at least I'll always have Mom."

Daddy and Lynn came and leaned against the fence beside us. Lynn climbed up on the fence, giving Diana's neck a squeeze. Diana leaned close to her.

"Hey, Steph, since you hurt your leg, don't worry about riding," Daddy said.

I smiled. "I'm goin' to. I want to."

"Are you sure?"

"Only if you promise not to act like a total geek, Dad."

"Oh, you mean act like I'm Clint Eastwood or something?" Daddy acted like he was drawing pistols from a holster. "'Tell me, do you feel lucky?'"

"That's what I mean," I said.

"Exactly," Diana said about one second later, rolling her eyes at me.

"What was that line? 'C'mon, make my day!'"

"That was from *Dirty Harry*, Norm," said Lynn. "That wasn't a Western."

"Oh, right. My bad." Daddy grinned. "Just call me the Norminator."

"Stop it, Daddy!"

Maggie came out of the barn leading Copper. Diana jumped from the fence and ran over to him. He lowered his head and poked her gently, right in the chest.

"Don't let him get out of line," Maggie said. "I know you're capable of keeping him in his place, and I expect you to do it." She gave Diana a pointed look.

"I will," Diana said. She started adjusting her own stirrups, and Maggie went back in the barn. A minute later she came back leading Sam. "Here's your buddy, Stephanie."

I looked at Sam's gigantic head, and my heart gave a little flutter despite the time we'd been spending together in the barn. His brown eyes looked nearly as big as softballs. And those long, square teeth. And omigosh, his hooves were the size of buckets. But then he swung his head around and nuzzled Maggie like a great big dog, and Maggie bumped heads with him, stroking his muzzle. "He is a very sweet fella."

I turned the sugar cube over in my hand and slid down from the fence. When I put weight on my foot my leg hurt pretty bad, but I ignored it and crossed the ring to Sam's side. I didn't like all that dust I was scuffing up, but I just took deep breaths and got to Sam and ran my hand slowly down the smooth bony surface of his big, trusting face, the way Maggie showed me yesterday.

"Thanks," I said to Maggie. Mama would poke fun at her long braid and her ancient jeans made soft with horse dirt. But not me.

Sam blinked and nudged me, which knocked me off-kilter, but I caught myself. I held out the sugar cube with my palm flat the way I'd seen Diana do it. The skin of Sam's muzzle, soft as fuzz on a baby's head, tickled me. I glanced at Diana. Hot liquid sugar dripped onto my palm.

"Oooh." I quickly wiped my hand off on the back of my jeans.

"I knew the slobber would get you," Diana said, laughing.

"Can you reach the stirrups?" Maggie asked. "Do you want help getting on?"

Daddy started across the ring, but I shook my head.

"I'll try by myself." I reached up and grasped the saddle horn, the way I'd seen Diana and Maggie do it, and raised my right foot way up to put it into the stirrup.

"Up and over!" Maggie said.

I pulled myself up, up, up Sam's huge round side until I was hanging there, one foot dangling.

"Throw your other leg over!" Diana said.

I did, even though it hurt like crazy. And in a minute I was sitting on top of Sam, my legs around his enormous sides.

Sam shifted his weight under me. I tightened my grip on the reins. Then Sam gave one ear a twitch, and it dawned on me that he might be saying "Hello." I patted his smooth, muscular neck, grinning at Diana, who was giving me a thumbs-up sign. Daddy and Lynn were smiling at me and so was Nick. A little knot inside me relaxed.

In the last two days, I had been brave. Time and again I had found courage that I didn't usually have. Aunt Lana, my youth group teacher, might tell me that courage came from God. If that was the case, I was grateful for it.

23

DIANA

As our car headed down the mountainside, I faced the window so no one would see my tears. Saying goodbye to Copper had been awful. I'd wanted to stand there and rub his sweet little dished-in head forever. "You'll move up in the pecking order," I'd whispered to him. Copper had butted my shoulder and dripped sugar slobber on my neck, which combined with the wet mess of my tears.

Moronic Mood-o-Meter in negative territory.

Just before we left, I sat on the fence and watched

Maggie release the horses to the mountain pasture. All fifty of them thundered from the enclosure, no saddles or bridles, tails flying, their bare-muscled bodies shining in the sun. They pounded by like a freight train, quarter horse and Appaloosa, Palomino and Arabian. Shoulder to shoulder, all wanting to be first. They streaked across the pasture, cavorting like little kids during recess.

Copper was so happy he bucked a few times just for the fun of it. I laughed out loud. I'd stayed there long after they lowered their heads and fell into the quiet tail-swishing rhythm of grazing.

As our car rounded a corner, I got a final glimpse of High Mist Ranch. Now I swallowed nervously as Norm pulled up in front of the Mountain Mist Companion Hospital and cut the engine.

Mom patted Norm's arm. "We made it." She looked back and smiled at me. I crossed my fingers and then hid them by sliding them underneath my thighs. My stomach hurt a little, mostly because I'd started taking my pills again, but being nervous didn't help. I looked over at Stephanie, who raised her eyebrows and tightened her lips.

Please be alive.

We trooped inside the waiting room. It was a crowded Saturday morning. A blond woman sat waiting with a golden retriever. A girl and her grandfather sat with a high-strung black-and-white terrier that kept barking and twirling in circles. A guy in his twenties had a small cage on the seat next to him with a terrified tabby cat crouched inside.

A tall, dark-haired woman wearing a surgical shirt came out. She had on a pin that said "Will Bite," and I thought it was funny. I wanted to ask her for one. She saw us standing there and said, "Hi, can I help you?"

"We came to see how the wolf is doing," Mom said. "This is Diana and Stephanie. They helped Doc do the surgery."

"Oh, yeah! They were a couple of troopers. I'm Kristi. Come on back and see for yourselves."

We followed Kristi down the narrow hall to the kennel area.

"Doc's on an office call. He'll come back and say hi later if he can." Kristi pointed us into a large room with a series of narrow runs. "Down near the end on the left," she said. "And don't be letting anybody out again, okay?" She smiled at Stephanie and me, but her eyes were dead serious. She left.

The dogs in the kennel knew someone was there. The noise was incredible. There was a bellow from one run, a whine from another, followed by a bunch of yelps. Jumping bodies slammed against metal cage doors. Toenails pummeled the cement floor. From the cat ward across the hall came a series of pitiful meows.

"How could a person stand to work here?" asked Norm.

"It's awful." Stephanie put her hands over her ears.

"I wish I could take every one of them home," said Mom.

"Me, too," I said.

I headed with Mom into the kennel. Norm and Stephanie followed. I walked the length of the room, passing a sad-eyed basset hound and a yipping, fluffy red Pomeranian that curled its lip and showed its sharp teeth.

"Amazing to think that all these incredibly different-looking dogs are related to wolves," said Mom.

"Yeah," I said. I let Mom put her arm over my shoulders, and when she intertwined her fingers with mine, I didn't pull away. I'd always remember what Mom had said to Norm. No one could ever take my place.

We found Waya's cage with Waya bandaged but alert, her head on Russell's knee. Russell was lying curled on the floor of the run, asleep. "He probably slept here last night," I whispered.

"Yeah, he did." Doc's voice came from behind us. Doc removed his cream-colored rubber exam gloves and pushed his wire rims up his nose.

Russell stirred in his sleep, his dark hair flopping over his eyes. His hand rested on Waya's neck.

"Has anyone seen Oginali?" I asked.

"No," Doc said. "I've been hoping we would. I read about these two wolves once, a brother and a sister, who were inseparable. The brother died, and the sister wouldn't leave his body. Everybody thought Oginali would follow Waya. But so far nothing. So, the pundits were officially wrong."

We watched Waya in silence. I thought about how Stephanie had gone with me that night and did a lot of things she was really scared to do. She hadn't ditched me, even though I'd tried to ditch her.

"Anyway," Doc continued, "Waya's doing well. I'm going to take the bandage off in three more days. She's a lucky girl."

"We came to pay for Waya's surgery," I said.

Doc nodded. "About that. I have a proposal for you. Because of the circumstances, I'm not going to charge Joe for that surgery. I told him I want to buy her instead. I made him a good offer, and I guess I caught him at a good time because he took it. As soon as Waya is able to travel, I plan to take her to a wolf rescue operation. And who knows, maybe we'll find Oginali by then. I'd like you to send your money to them to help care for her. Kristi can give you their address. Will you promise to do that?"

"Yessir! That's fantastic!" I said.

"That's great!" Stephanie said.

"Then it's settled. Our code in medicine is 'Do no harm.' While you did quite a bit of harm by releasing the wolves, I believe you at least partially rectified it with your excellent assistance in surgery. How's that?"

"That's more than fair," said Mom. "Thanks, Doc."

Doc tightened his ponytail. "We aim to please." Doc shook Stephanie's hand. "How's your leg?" he asked. "Mr. Morgan tells me you put a hurting on that trap of his." Doc grinned.

Stephanie blushed. "Uh, yeah. My leg's going to be okay. But could I ask ... what do you think will happen to Oginali?"

Doc shrugged. "No telling. If she kills chickens, she could get herself shot. Or poisoned. Maybe I'll get a chance to put a saving on her. If she wanders off deeper into the mountains, she'll have to learn to hunt on her own. Maybe she will. Maybe she'll try to find Waya. Most likely, though, we'll never see Oginali again." Doc glanced at his watch. Held out his hand to shake mine. "Diana, maybe there's a future for you in veterinary medicine. The animals of the world need all the friends they can get. Take care."

I could feel myself blush. Doc shook Mom and Norm's hands and then hurried out.

"We better hit the road," said Norm. "It's a long trip."

"Can I just have one minute to say good-bye?" I asked.

"Sure, sweetie. We'll be out in the car," Mom said. "Be careful."

Mom, Norm, and Stephanie left, and I unlocked the door of the cage. Russell's eyelids trembled but his eyes were still closed. His breathing was slow and even. A pair of topaz eyes followed me as I opened the cage door and stepped inside. I examined the tight, broad bandage wrapped around Waya's chest. Slowly, I knelt.

I looked into those golden eyes. I saw wariness and fear, but also curiosity and hope. I reached out to stroke Waya's head and remembered Maggie's story about the wolves inside.

Waya's eyes narrowed and her lip curled back, showing curved yellow teeth. My heart skipped, but I offered my hand to the wolf. Long hushed seconds swept by. Waya's black nostrils quivered. Then she stretched out her neck and licked my palm.

"Good-bye," I whispered. "Bye, Russell," I added, with a squeezing of my heart.

Russell opened his eyes. I noticed, for the first time, that they were deep amber, like Waya's. He didn't say anything.

I let the words tumble out. "I wanted to tell you something. I dreamed about Oginali last night. I had a dream with this amazing blue background, where I was running beside Oginali through the woods, high in the mountains, and Oginali was hunting, and her eyes were like gold and her tail was like this flag, waving really high. I dreamed she wasn't scared anymore."

Russell's eyes flared. He looked like he might say something, but then turned his face away.

"Thanks for trying to be my friend." I waited a minute and then stepped outside the cage and shut the gate. I felt in my pocket for the bullet Doc had given me. Maybe if I gave Russell some time and wrote him a letter, he'd answer. I'd try.

I went outside and climbed into the car. Mom smiled, reached over to the backseat, and squeezed my hand very tight.

As the car went down the mountain, our whole family stared out the window and scanned the shifting forest shadows for signs of Oginali. Finally, my pills got to me, and I slept in the car, dreaming again of Oginali running over mountains, through valleys, growing stronger and fiercer. In my dream Oginali's salt and pepper coat thickened as summer turned to fall. When she reached the ridge where the water turned west— the Continental Divide—she bounded on without fear. In my dream, when Waya, all healed up, arrived at the wolf rescue, Oginali was already there. Waiting.

Talk It Up!

Want free books?
First looks at the best new fiction?
Awesome exclusive merchandise?

We want to hear from you!

Give us your opinions on titles, covers, and stories.
Join the Z Street Team.

Email us at zstreetteam@zondervan.com
to sign up today!

Also—Friend us on Facebook!

www.facebook.com/goodteenreads

- Video Trailers
- Connect with your favorite authors
- Sneak peeks at new releases
- Giveaways
- Fun discussions
- And much more!